PENGU

A TOUCH

Jonathan Coe was born in Birmingham in 1961. His most recent novel is *The Rain Before It Falls*. He is also the author of *The Accidental Woman*, *A Touch of Love*, *The Dwarves of Death*, *What a Carve Up!*, which won the 1995 John Llewellyn Rhys Prize, *The House of Sleep*, which won the 1998 Prix Médicis Étranger, *The Rotters' Club*, winner of the Everyman Wodehouse Prize, and *The Closed Circle*. His biography of the novelist B.S. Johnson, *Like a Fiery Elephant*, won the 2005 Samuel Johnson Prize for best non-fiction book of the year. He lives in London with his wife and two children.

A Touch of Love

JONATHAN COE

PENGUIN BOOKS

PENGUIN BOOKS

Published by the Penguin Group
Penguin Books Ltd, 80 Strand, London WC2R 0RL, England
Penguin Group (USA) Inc., 375 Hudson Street, New York, New York 10014, USA
Penguin Group (Canada), 90 Eglinton Avenue East, Suite 700, Toronto, Ontario, Canada M4P 2Y3
(a division of Pearson Penguin Canada Inc.)
Penguin Ireland, 25 St Stephen's Green, Dublin 2, Ireland (a division of Penguin Books Ltd)
Penguin Group (Australia), 250 Camberwell Road, Camberwell, Victoria 3124, Australia
(a division of Pearson Australia Group Pty Ltd)
Penguin Books India Pvt Ltd, 11 Community Centre, Panchsheel Park, New Delhi – 110 017, India
Penguin Group (NZ), 67 Apollo Drive, Rosedale, North Shore 0632, New Zealand
(a division of Pearson New Zealand Ltd)
Penguin Books (South Africa) (Pty) Ltd, 24 Sturdee Avenue,
Rosebank, Johannesburg 2196, South Africa

Penguin Books Ltd, Registered Offices: 80 Strand, London WC2R 0RL, England

www.penguin.com

First published by Gerald Duckworth and Co. Ltd 1989
First published in Penguin Books in 2000
This edition published 2008
1

Copyright © Jonathan Coe, 1989
All rights reserved

Typeset by Intype London Ltd
Printed in England by Clays Ltd, St Ives plc

ISBN: 978-0-141-03331-0

www.greenpenguin.co.uk

Penguin Books is committed to a sustainable future
for our business, our readers and our planet.
The book in your hands is made from paper
certified by the Forest Stewardship Council.

Contents

Note

I'd like to thank Michèle O'Leary for making it possible for me to write about a lawyer; and Pip Lattey for introducing me to the work of Simone Weil, which came to influence this book.

The manuscript was read at various stages by different friends, all of whom were helpful; but two people were especially generous with their support and criticism. They were Nuala Murray (on the first half) and Ralph Pite (on the second). My thanks to them, and also, belatedly, to Anna Haycraft, whose suggestions were both far-reaching and valuable.

The quotation on pages 223–4 is from *Gravity and Grace*, by Simone Weil, translated by Emma Craufurd and published by Routledge & Kegan Paul Ltd.

PART ONE

The Meeting of Minds

Thursday 17th April, 1986

'Darling, don't be silly, of course there isn't going to be a nuclear war.

. . .

'I'm just approaching Junction 21. Should be in Coventry in about twenty minutes. I've got to call in at the university.

. . .

'Well, forget what he said. He doesn't know what he's talking about. The world is run by sane and sensible people, just like you and me.

. . .

'I miss you too. Kiss Peter for me. And tell him I –

. . .

'What? No, some maniac pulled out straight in front of me. Some of these people are doing at least ninety. I don't know why the police don't catch them.

. . .

'I don't know if I've got time to call on him. Not if I want to be home tonight.

. . .

'Anyway, what would I say to him? I haven't seen him for years. I can barely remember what he looks like.

. . .

'No, I don't see why we should let him use our holiday cottage. We bought it for us, not for letting out to strangers.

. . .

'What do you mean, he sounded peculiar?

. . .

'Darling, he doesn't know what he's talking about. And neither do you. Libya, Syria, America, Russia – it's a very complicated situation. If you really think the world is going to be plunged into war, then . . . well, I'll come home, obviously.

. . .

'All right, give me his address.

. . .

'Yes, I'll pop in this evening when I've been to the university. It means I probably won't be home till ten. Maybe later. No, I can find it, I've got an A to Z.

. . .

'Now don't panic. Don't watch the news if it's upsetting you. Forget he said it.

. . .

'I'll explain to him about the cottage. I doubt if there's anything wrong, really. Perhaps he's just been working too hard. You know how it is with students, they do nothing for weeks and then they stay up until all hours.

. . .

'Don't worry. I will.

. . .

'You too.

. . .

'Kiss kiss.'

★

Ted came off at Junction 21 and joined the M69. The important thing, as he had come to realize, was to maintain good relations with clients. He had little hope of making a new sale at the university but it was some weeks since he had spoken to Dr Fowler and he wanted to check that the new system had been working properly. After glancing ahead to see that the middle lane was clear, he allowed his eyes to flick across to the passenger seat, and to the file in which he recorded the personal details of his customers. With his left hand he turned the pages until he reached the letter F. Fowler, Dr Stephen. Married, two children: Paul and Nicola. Nicola had had a dental appointment on the 24th of March. Two extractions. This would give him something to start off with. ('Steve! Good to see you again. Just thought I'd pop in. You know, in the area and all that. How's the wife and kids? Nicky's teeth aren't still giving her trouble, I hope? Good. Glad to hear it . . .')

He arrived on campus shortly before five, but Dr Fowler had gone home. A note on his door said that he would be available for consultation the next morning.

Ted took a circuitous route back to the car park, surprised to find himself enjoying the late sunshine and the unaccustomed experience of being surrounded by people younger than himself. When he reached the car he did not get inside, but sat on the bonnet and looked around him. He had been preparing himself for his encounter with Dr Fowler with the single-mindedness which had recently, for the second time running, won him the firm's coveted 'Salesman of the Year' award, so it was only now that he was able to give Katharine's phone call any serious thought. The prospects it raised were not pleasant. He had no real wish to see Robin again: if he had, he would have called on him before, on one of his many visits to the university. Least of all did he want to be put in the position of having to look after him, if, as Katharine had suggested, there was something seriously wrong.

Then again, she was always exaggerating.

Ted did not like to approach a situation unarmed; and part of his unease, he realized, could be ascribed to insufficiency of data. Seeing Robin again, knowing nothing about how he had spent the last four years, would be like meeting a stranger.

He thought for a while, and then took out his file and opened it at the letter G. The pages flapped gently in the breeze. Soon he had put down everything he could remember about his old friend.

Grant, Robin.

Graduated from Cambridge, 1981.

Last saw him at wedding, 1982.

Have been sending him Christmas cards and family newsletters (NB is this how he knows about our cottage?).

Family: mother and father, one sister.

Now working on thesis – and has been for 4 (?) years.

Said to be sounding 'peculiar' and 'depressed'.

Says he needs a holiday.

Violent reaction to the events of the last two days: says that the bombers should not have been sent into Libya.

Ted laid down his pen, frowned and began to feel even more gloomy. People could change a lot in four years. He hoped that Robin hadn't gone all political.

*

As he entered the south-western suburbs of Coventry, Ted stopped to consult his A to Z and found that the relevant page was missing. The spine of the book had cracked and he had been meaning to replace it for more than a month: he had only himself to blame. The only course of action, it seemed, was to ask a stranger for directions. Meanwhile he was not averse to driving at random through these tree-lined avenues, looking at the houses and listening appreciatively to birdsong as it mingled with the music of his practised gear changes. Anything to put off the moment of arrival.

After a few minutes, and after passing several pedestrians who did not, for various irrational reasons, strike him as prepossessing, he caught sight of a young woman walking rapidly ahead on his side of the road, with her back to his car. He drew up beside her and pipped the horn. The woman started and turned; and Ted was dismayed to find that she was Indian. Now he would probably have difficulty making himself understood. But it was too late to do anything about that; she was already approaching his open window.

'Yes?' she said, fiercely.

He was looking into a pair of strong wide hostile eyes. For a moment he was thrown off guard, suddenly conscious of an intense, vivid personality in confrontation with his own. Unable to hold her gaze, he looked down and noticed, for the first time, that a button had gone missing from his left cuff.

'I was wondering if you could tell me,' he began, 'how to find – ' and he named the street where Robin lived.

'Where?' said the woman: more, Ted might have noticed, in surprise than in incomprehension.

'Here.' He fumbled with his file, and found the address which he had scribbled down on a piece of paper after pulling over to the hard shoulder at the end of his conversation with Katharine. He showed it to her.

'I've just come from there,' she said. 'Are you going to see Robin?'

'Yes.'

'It's round the corner just behind you. I hope you get more joy out of him than I did.'

She turned and walked away, her hands in her pockets, pulling her coat tightly around her even though the evening was still warm. Ted was silenced, at first, but managed within a few seconds to lean out of his window and call after her:

'Robin Grant? You know him? Are you a friend of his?'

The woman did not stop, or slow down, or even raise her voice; in fact her reply was barely audible.

'How should I know?'

Ted watched her receding figure until his eyes glazed over. He was numb with confusion. Then, slowly and more reluctantly than ever, he performed a three-point turn and drove up the side street which she had indicated.

The address on his piece of paper referred to a tall grey terraced house, shabbily painted and separated from the pavement only by a bleak strip of untended garden. Ted got out of his car and locked the door. The street was quiet, dappled with the kindly glow of the evening sun. Slinging his jacket over his shoulder, loosening his tie, he stepped boldly up to the front door and rang the bell marked 'Grant, R.'.

For some time nothing happened. Then there was the distant sound of an opening door, footsteps, a shadow behind the frosted glass and finally, as the door opened, a pallid, unfamiliar, unshaven face.

'Robin?'

'Come on in.'

'You phoned Katharine. Did she tell you I was coming?'

'Yes. Come on in.'

Wordlessly Robin led him out of the light down a gloomy hallway, past the bottom of a steep staircase, and through a door to the right. Inside his flat it was even darker: the curtains were drawn and the air was dry and smoky. Once Ted's eyes had adjusted to the darkness he took in the details of a sparsely furnished bedsitting room, with an unmade bed against one wall, clothes scattered over the floor, two bookcases filled to bursting point, and a desk, which was empty except for a biro and three small red notebooks, piled one on top of the other. On the mantel-piece was a radio tuned to Radio Four: an emotionless male voice was reporting the day's events in Tripoli and at Westminster.

'Were you not expecting me so soon?' Ted asked.

'I'm sorry. I lost track of the time. Do sit down.'

He revealed a sofa by sweeping a pile of shirts and underpants to the floor.

'Well, Robin,' said Ted, looking at him and wondering why he was not properly dressed (he was wearing only a red towel dressing gown and a pair of slippers), 'we meet in altered circumstances.'

'How is Kate?' he asked.

'Oh, she's fine. Just fine. A funny thing,' he announced, to break the immediate embarrassed silence, ' – I stopped to ask for directions just now and spoke to a friend of yours.'

'Oh?'

'Yes. She seemed slightly . . . Asian.'

'Her name's Aparna.'

'Striking-looking woman, I thought. She'd just been to visit you, too, had she?'

'Yes.'

'Well, you don't seem to be short of friends, Robin.'

'We quarrelled.'

'Oh? Nothing serious, I hope?'

'Yes, it was. It was about a book.'

There was another silence. Ted, master of the manipulative conversation, adept at the winning of confidences, was finding it hard to cope with the listless minimalism of Robin's answers. Fortunately, however, there was a sudden change of subject.

'Anyway, Ted, I spoke to Kate on the phone about your cottage and she didn't seem to think there'd be any problem. I suppose you've brought the keys with you?'

Ted was too nonplussed to respond. Robin sat down on the bed opposite him and continued (his voice cold, effortful, inexpressive):

'You know, if I hadn't had the chance to go away somewhere, I think I would have gone mad. Or something. I've been feeling so tired. I think I must need some sleep. I think I must need some rest. I feel as though I need to talk. I need to see someone. I need to get away. I need to be alone. I feel frightened. I don't know what I'm doing. I don't know what I have been doing, these last few days. I don't know where I've been. I went into a shop. I picked up a tube of toothpaste, and walked out with it. The woman had to run after me. She said, You haven't paid for that. I've hurt my finger. I slipped and hurt it on the stairs. I feel exhausted. I feel cold and hungry. I'm always hungry. I put a frozen pie in the oven, and came back half an hour later, but I hadn't put the oven on. I'd forgotten. I had to eat bread instead. I can't believe what I've been hearing on the radio. She let him use our air bases. They used our air bases to bomb Libya. I'm scared. I've got to get away. And I've always wanted to go back to the Lakes. It's quiet up there, and clean, and it has associations for me. I used to go up there with my family. My parents and my sister. One of the things I've been thinking, the last few days, is how much I miss my family. How stupid it is to cut myself off from them like this. If I hadn't been able to use your cottage, I was going to write to them, ask them if I could go back home, stay with them a while. But this will be better. Much better.'

A softer man than Ted might have been moved by this speech. Indeed, at a pinch, Ted himself might have been moved, if he had been listening. Instead he was surveying the squalor of Robin's flat, and thinking about his cottage in the Lake District, and as he did so, his resolve hardened. They had bought the cottage with a legacy from Katharine's mother, who had died in 1983. The question of what they should do with the money had been the subject of several long and violent arguments, which he now recalled with some fondness. Eventually he had had his way, and the Lakes had won out over Cornwall. Physical force had not been necessary, after all. The cottage was on the main road between Torver and Coniston; all that stood between it and a fine view of the water was half a mile of dense pine forest. Ted and Katharine had been conscious, at first, that their presence might be regarded by the locals as invasive, but they had had no difficulty in integrating themselves into the community: their only neighbours, the Burnets, who lived across the road, turned out to be a charming couple from Harrow who were always ready to make up a four at bridge. Ted was not prepared to have his standing among these people compromised by the arrival of this disreputable acquaintance who clearly had no idea of how to look after property. His eye – so used to monitoring Katharine's efforts – had soon picked out the grime caked on to Robin's skirting board, the ash on the carpet, the cobwebs hanging in unvisited corners. Not that he could give this as his reason for refusing, of course. A little white lie would have to be invented.

'Well, the fact is, Robin,' he said, 'that Katharine was being somewhat premature. What she seems to have forgotten is that my mother is staying there at the moment. She'll be staying there for a month at least.'

Robin stared at him in absolute silence, his expression blank, his eyes unmoving. Ted wondered whether he had heard, or registered, or understood his explanation, which had come out, he thought, sounding very reasonable. He tried to phrase a question – 'Is that all right?', 'You do see the problem, don't you?' – but the words would not form. What he heard himself ask, finally, was:

'Now – what about something to eat?'

*

It transpired that there was no food in the kitchen, apart from some margarine and half a packet of flaccid cream crackers. Ted went out to find a chip shop. Not having visited a chip shop for several years, he was surprised to be charged more than three pounds. The owner told him that such prices were quite common now, even in the north. When he returned to the flat, he found that Robin had not fetched clean cutlery and warmed the plates, as requested, but was sitting at his desk writing a letter.

'I'm sorry,' he said. 'I didn't expect you back so soon.'

Ted sent him off to the kitchen and took advantage of his absence by having a surreptitious look at the letter. It was to his mother, and began:

This will probably come as a surprise to you but I am thinking of coming home and perhaps staying for a little while. I hope this idea appeals to you because I know we haven't communicated much recently, but I've been thinking how nice it would be to see you both again. I seem to have taken a lot of wrong turnings recently and I badly need to get away from here and think things through. I haven't put that very well, but I shall try to explain things more . . .

This was all he had written. Ted was reading over the letter a second time, puzzled, when Robin came back. Anxious not to be thought inquisitive, he pretended to have been looking at the red notebooks.

'What's in these?' he asked, pointing.

'Stories,' said Robin. He handed Ted a lukewarm plate and a knife and fork.

'You're still writing, then, are you?'

'On and off.'

'I still have that issue of the college magazine,' said Ted, in a tone of chuckling reminiscence. 'You know, the one we both contributed to? You wrote a story, and I did a short article.'

'I don't remember.'

'My piece was about object-oriented programming. People told me it was rather humorous.'

Robin shook his head and began to eat chips with his fingers.

'So what are these stories about?'

'Oh,' said Robin, wearily, 'it's just a sequence I've been working on. I don't know why I bother, really. There are four stories, all interrelated. They're about sex and friendship and choices and things like that.'

'Four?' said Ted. 'I can only see three.'

'Aparna has one of them. I wanted her to read it: she borrowed it this afternoon.' He pulled apart a piece of cod and took one or two reluctant mouthfuls. Then he added, suddenly: 'One should think very carefully before speaking. Don't you agree?'

'Pardon?'

'I said, one should think very carefully before speaking.'

'How do you mean?'

He was leaning forward, newly earnest and communicative.

'What I mean is, a word can be a lethal weapon.' He paused on this phrase, apparently pleased with it. 'One word can destroy the work of a million others. A misplaced word can undo anything: a family, a marriage, a friendship.'

Ted was about to ask him why he thought he knew anything about marriage, but decided against it.

'I'm not with you,' he said.

'I was just thinking how easy it was to upset Aparna today. You see, she showed me this book.' He pushed his plate aside, once and for all. 'It was a new book, a hardback. I could see it wasn't a library book, so I started teasing her about it, saying, "Since when have people like us been able to afford books like that?" Then she told me she'd been given it, because one of the authors was a friend of hers. So I took the book and looked at the title page, and there were two names, one of them English and one Indian. So I pointed at the Indian name and said, I suppose this is your friend? And she stared at me and slowly took the book out of my hand, and she said, "You just gave away a lot about yourself".'

Ted was baffled. He thought carefully and fast, anxious not to embarrass himself. What was the matter with this man, that they misunderstood each other so often? Friendship, he had always believed, was a meeting of minds, like marriage. Katharine and he not only understood each other as soon as they spoke, but frequently they understood each other even before they spoke. Sometimes he knew what she was thinking even before she had said it. Often she knew what he was going to think even before he had begun to think it. Intellectual compatibility had become one of the constants of his life, one of the givens, a habit, an assumption, like the company car, like the greenhouse – for which, he now remembered, he was meant to be buying three new panes at the weekend.

What was the purpose of this abstruse anecdote? Presumably it hinged on the fact that one of the authors of this book was Indian, and that Aparna was for some reason offended at being linked with her. But surely Aparna was herself Indian? She had a funny-sounding name. Her skin was, not to put too fine a point on it, dark. So was her hair. She didn't have a red spot in the middle of her forehead, admittedly, but that could probably be explained away.

Why should one Indian not wish to be associated with another Indian, simply because they were both Indian?

He put this question to Robin, as best he could.

'It's not that simple,' said Robin. 'You see, I've known her now for four years. She's been here ever since I've been here. She's been here longer than that. Six, seven years.' His speech was halting, now, as if he had lost the habit of explaining things to people. 'When she got here she was proud of her nationality. She even showed it off. The way you saw her dressed today – she didn't always use to dress like that. She was popular, too, in those days: so popular that it used to make me jealous. Of course, she always had time for me. We were very close, in some ways. But still, I'd be standing talking to her outside the library and every few seconds someone would be coming by, saying hello, stopping to chat. It would be as much as I could do to get a word in edgeways. Not just students, either: professors, lecturers, librarians, the people from the canteen. You wouldn't believe it. What you saw today was a shadow. She lives alone now. In a tower block, right on the other side of town. The fourteenth floor. I'm the only one she still sees. They've all forgotten her. They got bored with her.'

There descended a silence which was, it seemed to Ted, potentially interminable.

'So?' he asked.

'Racism doesn't have to be blatant. It doesn't have to be sudden, either, and it can happen anywhere. She got tired of being thought of as foreign; she got tired that it was always the first thing people noticed about her. She only came here to work, and get her degree, and then she found that people had decided to use her to brighten up their lives. "Their bit of local colour" she used to call it. She fought hard to be taken seriously, but it hasn't worked. And now she thinks that even I'm no different. Even I think of her that way. She's so bitter now, with me and with everybody; and yet I can remember this kindness, this warmth, that I never found in anyone else.'

Ted, who had no idea of what to say to any of this, began to clear up the plates.

'Do you ever feel,' said Robin, 'that you've gone through your whole life making the wrong decisions? Or worse still, that you've never really *made* any decisions? You can see that there were times when you might have been able to – help someone, for instance, but you never had the courage to do it? Yes?'

Ted paused at the doorway to the kitchen, and said: 'You're not really on top form at the moment, are you, Robin?'

Robin followed him through and watched as he put the plates into the sink.

'Or even worse than that, have you ever wondered what's the point of making decisions in the first place, when the world's run by maniacs, and we're all at the mercy of interests outside our control, and we never know when something terrible might happen, like a war or something?'

'Well, you're absolutely right, of course. Look, Robin,'

Ted turned, and said, unexpectedly, 'you haven't got a needle and thread, have you? I've lost a button.'

'Yes. In the drawer of the dressing table.'

They went back into the other room. Ted found the needle and a reel of white cotton, and began threading it.

'Keep talking,' he said. 'I'm listening to every word you say.'

'I just feel . . . I need to get away and start all over again. Do you ever have that feeling?'

'Sometimes.' The needle had a very small eye, and Ted was finding it difficult to get started.

'I mean, I just don't know where the last few years have gone. I seem to have achieved nothing, personally, academically, creatively. I seem to have lost all direction.'

'Yes, I see.' He tried sucking the end of the cotton, hoping that this would make it easier to thread.

'I never see my family. I never hear from my sister any more. There are no jobs in universities these days. I can't see where my thesis is leading. My relationships with women have been disastrous. I can only see the negative side of things. Everything seems flawed. Everything seems useless and futile. Do you understand what that feels like?'

Ted, having succeeded in threading the needle, and having found a spare button in the pocket of his shirt, was now taking his shirt off. It was halfway over his head as he answered:

'Carry on. I know what you mean.'

'I've been reading this book. It's . . . well, I think it's clarified a few things about what I may be going through.

This woman, she talks a lot about the "I", the importance of the "I".'

'The importance of the eye?'

'The "I". One letter. The – the sense of personal identity. You know, your sense of self, the person you are.'

'Yes, quite.' Ted tutted. He had not tied a proper knot, the cotton had come adrift, and now he was going to have to start all over again.

'Are you listening?'

'Of course I'm listening. Do you mind if I put the light on a minute? I'm having a few problems here.'

'Well, what do you think?' he asked, as Ted got up to switch the light on.

'What do I think?'

'What do you think I should do?'

'Well – ' Ted started sucking on the cotton again, and said, 'perhaps the problem is that you're lonely. Have you thought about getting a girlfriend?'

'What?'

'You know, someone who could keep this flat tidy, and provide you with a bit of company in the evening. Not someone like Aparna, who'd only argue all the time. Someone stable and supportive.'

'And where would that get me?'

Ted caught the note of contempt in his voice and, although he was engaged in tying another knot, looked up. He said, very seriously: 'I know one thing, Robin. I was never really happy before I married Katharine.'

Robin avoided his eyes.

'I never want to be involved with a woman again,' he said, and left the room.

Ted put down the needle, considered these words, and made a mental note to write them down in his file for future reference; for they confirmed, or rather reawakened, a personal theory which he had once entertained regarding Robin. In fact it had been Katharine herself who first suggested it, back at Cambridge. 'Don't be stupid,' he had said at the time, 'Robin is as normal as you or I'. Gradually, however, the idea had come to seem less incredible, and Ted had overcome his initial revulsion. In an odd way it had even reconciled him to the closeness of Robin's friendship with Katharine, to the obvious pleasure which they took in each other's company. Towards the end of their last summer term, the three of them were scarcely to be seen apart. And Katharine had said to him once: 'It would explain why he is so sensitive.'

'Sensitive?'

'Yes. They're always the most sensitive.'

He had asked Robin, subsequently, whether he thought that this was true, that they were always the most sensitive, and he had said yes, it was often the case, and had added that some of the people he most admired were homosexual; which struck Ted, then, as being a shocking admission. But he had told himself, Never mind, he is simply less fortunate than the rest of us, and this display of liberalism had been the cause of much private self-congratulation. It had its limits, of course. For instance, he would never have left Robin alone in a room with Peter. Ted believed that you couldn't be too careful, where children were concerned.

Robin came back, and opened the curtains at the window by his desk. The sky was darkening.

'I suppose you'll have to be getting back soon.'

'Well, I've been thinking about that,' said Ted. He had been thinking, in fact, that it would suit him to call on Dr Fowler the next morning; in which case, he wouldn't have to visit this dreary part of the world again for more than a month. And he had been thinking, distasteful as he found the ambience of Robin's flat, that here at least was the chance of a bed for the night. 'You don't seem too grand and there's no real reason why I have to be home tonight. Why don't I phone Katharine and tell her I won't be back until tomorrow?'

'If you like,' said Robin.

This was not the flood of gratitude that Ted had anticipated.

'Then maybe we could go out for a drink. Do you think that would cheer you up? And perhaps I could read one of these stories of yours.'

'All right. I'll get dressed.'

Robin took the least dirty of his clothes into the kitchen and changed while Ted was on the telephone. He returned in time to hear the last few words of the conversation.

'Who's Peter?' he asked.

'Peter? Surely I must have mentioned him, in one of the newsletters. Our first boy. Two years old.'

'Oh. Of course.'

23

'Yes . . .' Ted smiled. 'He's a grand little chap.'

Robin picked up the first of the notebooks and slipped it into the pocket of his trousers.

'Let's go if we're going,' he said.

★

It is a warm night in mid-April; getting on for eleven o'clock. Robin and Ted have left the pub, and are setting off in a new direction, Robin leading, Ted hurrying to keep up. The people of Coventry are sleeping, now, or preparing to sleep; but they continue to walk at a breathless pace, these two friends who are no longer friends.

Up Mayfield Road, along Broadway, across the bowling green, scene of many of Robin's private reveries. Here he has sat, on windy spring Saturdays, watching husbands and wives pass their time in skilled and light-hearted competition, sporting anoraks and headscarves. Old people, still bound to one another, still bound to the city in which they have lived, worked, grown up; in which they were born. He has watched them on windy Saturday afternoons, feeling at once both contempt and envy. He has wished to join them, to demonstrate his own skill, for he, too, has played bowls, with his mother, father and sister. Naturally he'd be out of practice, a little erratic at first. And at the same time he has wished only to leave them, because he is burning from the touch of their scared occasional eyes, fleeting but eloquent glances which phrase, unmistakably,

24

the questions, Who is that strange man, and why is he staring at us?

Across the road and into Spencer Park. In autumn here the trees rustle, and you have to weave your way through kids playing football, with piles of clothes for goalposts. But tonight it is quiet and empty, except for a young woman out walking her dog: a bit foolhardy you might have thought, but perhaps she feels safe with the dog, an Alsatian after all, and a big one at that. She doesn't say hello, her eyes are averted. It is very still, once she has passed. And now the lights of the city are before them, beckoning them, these two companions who have nothing to offer each other in the way of companionship, and their stride quickens again.

Across the steel footbridge, and over the railway line. There are few trains at this time of night, services to London and Birmingham and Oxford have all but ceased, but now as they cross the footbridge a goods train passes beneath their feet. It seems immensely long and noisy, making conversation impossible. A good job, then, that they have no wish to converse, although a detached observer, supposing one were to pass by, might have noticed on Ted's face the marks of a growing unease, the strainings of a question long since framed but as yet unable to express itself. But Robin is oblivious to this nuance; he is chuckling in a secretive way at the graffiti which cover the walls of the bridge from top to bottom, from end to end. Anarchy – The Only Way Out. Say No To Cruise. I Have Seen The

Fnords. Disarm Rapists. So Much To Say, So Little Paint. Wogs Out. Nigger Shit. Something about this mixture seems to appeal to him, but the nature of this appeal clearly eludes his confidant (in whom he has no confidence), for Ted's sidelong glances grow more and more puzzled and wary. And sidelong. So that now they have given up all converse not only of the voices, but of the eyes.

Down Grosvenor Road, a deserted warehouse to their right, houses to their left, half of them boarded up. Soon they are walking through the subway and then into Warwick Road, past the lit windows of estate agents and the door of a crowded wine bar, from which people are beginning to emerge. Robin hesitates here briefly, but soon moves on, faster than ever. Ted stops and peers in confusion at the doorway, then runs to catch up. It occurs to him, not before time, that Robin has in mind, as the mainspring and primary motivation behind this walk, the consumption of further alcohol. He puts this question bluntly, and is answered with a nod and a noise. Robin now stops again, this time to look in the window of a bookshop. He ignores the main display of paperbacks and picture-books, concentrating his attention instead on a bulky volume half hidden towards the back, in a right-hand corner: *The Failure of Contemporary Literature*, by Leonard Davis. A sticker attached to the front cover announces, as a further inducement to prospective purchasers, that Professor Davis is a Local Author. Robin clicks his tongue.

The precinct is all but deserted. There is the occasional down-and-out, obviously, slumped in a doorway, but you get these even in the most prosperous cities. In fact you get them especially in the most prosperous cities. The precinct has a haunted air about it at this time of night. Built for public use, designed purposely to accommodate crowds of happy shoppers, thronging, swarming, threading in and out of Smiths, Habitat, Woolworths, BHS, Top Man, and yet tonight there are only these two figures, wordless, distant, their footsteps echoing in the concrete square, their shadows faint in the fluorescent light. Where are all the old women, dragging shopping bags on wheels? Where are the young couples, window-shopping, arm in arm? Where are the punks and skinheads? Tucked up in bed somewhere, I hope, in terraced houses or high-rise blocks, hundreds of feet up in the air. They would have received little attention from these two, tonight, anyway, because they are now walking faster still, and Robin has begun to glance anxiously at his watch.

They cut across Broadgate, past the statue of Lady Godiva, and head down Trinity Street. Ted has no way of knowing it, but they are not far from the cathedral; here, in the daytime, you can while away a pleasant hour or more, admiring the windows, looking at the Sutherland tapestry, or experiencing (for a small fee) the holographic recreation of the Blitz, an aural and visual adventure in three dimensions, for those who weren't lucky enough to have been present at the real thing. But Ted's only memory of the cathedral will be of a dark bulk rising to his right as he crosses the square, somewhere behind the old library. And even then he will not have known that it was the cathedral, because he is tired, and angry, and has stopped asking questions. Robin, needless to say, never ventures information unsolicited. Ted has long since ceased to feel any curiosity about his surroundings anyhow, and the whole city has begun to seem like a clammy inferno, one unsavoury district after another. He hardly notices, then, that they have left most of the shops behind, have just walked past the dimly-lit forecourt of a large, run-down hospital, almost uninhabited, it seems, at this hour, and that they have entered upon a long street composed mainly of bulky terraced houses. He does notice, however, that only about one in four of the people they have passed in the last few minutes has been white; and this gives him a certain anxiety.

Before long they have taken a right-hand turn, into a very dark side street. They stop at the door of what appears at first to be a house, in a row of houses. Through a glass panel in the door, a faint orange glow is visible. Then Ted realizes that there is a sign above the door, that the house has a name: that it is, in fact, another pub. Robin is knocking on the glass panel, rhythmically, like a code, and now a man has come to the door. A few words, and they are admitted.

*

'What's going on?' asked Ted.

They were seated in a small gloomy bar with perhaps a dozen other men, most of whom Robin seemed to know.

Everyone was absolutely silent, and the average age of the patrons, not counting Robin and Ted, was about sixty-two.

'A friend of mine told me about this place,' said Robin. 'They lock the front door and then let us stay until about three or four. The police know about it but they usually turn a blind eye.'

Ted was appalled.

'How often do you do this?'

'I don't know. A couple of nights a week.'

'You need the drink that badly?'

'It's not the drink. I can get that at home. It's the company.'

'The company!' He looked around in astonishment. 'But look at these people. They're old men. You have nothing in common with them. Nobody's even talking.'

'It's better than being alone.'

'But tonight I would have been with you.'

There was no reply to this remark, so Ted assumed that it had struck home. He noticed that he was drinking too fast, and had nearly finished the second of the gin and tonics which Robin had pressed upon him. When he had suggested going out for a drink, he had envisaged a convivial evening, drinking pints of lager in a boisterous, youthful environment. Now he felt bored and drunk and homesick. Robin was fingering an empty glass, his eyes half closed, slumped in his chair, his head bowed in a gesture of militant introversion.

'It seems to me,' said Ted, 'that you're overreacting to this little quarrel.'

'Quarrel?'

'Your argument with Aparna. I take it that that's why you're behaving in this way?'

He looked up and his eyes awoke, briefly.

'It's not the only thing,' he said.

Ted could see, none the less, that he had touched a nerve, and ditching his original theory about Robin he began to wonder whether there was more to this friendship than he had suspected. There was no point, he decided, in trying to approach the subject delicately; so he simply asked, 'Are you having an affair with her?'

Robin's stare was cold and enquiring. 'What makes you think that?'

'You mentioned having been close.'

'We are,' said Robin, but amended it to 'were'.

'And?'

'It was never physical. I suppose that's what you're getting at.'

'I see. A platonic friendship,' said Ted, drily.

'If you like.'

'A meeting of minds.'

Robin hesitated, then rose to his feet. Ted thought, for a moment, with a mixture of panic and relief, that he had taken offence and was about to leave; but he had merely stood up in order to fetch the red notebook out from the back pocket of his jeans.

'Since you've mentioned the phrase,' he said, 'why don't you read this story? Then you might have more idea what you're talking about.'

He threw the notebook down on the table and went to get two more drinks. After a while Ted picked the book up and looked apprehensively through its pages of small, untidy handwriting. He had read some of Robin's fiction at Cambridge, and not found it inspiring: in fact they still had one of his typescripts back at home. In their last term, shortly before Ted and Katharine announced their engagement, Robin had presented her with a story – inscribed rather fulsomely, in Ted's opinion. He had only ever managed to read the first half. Still, this appeared to be considerably shorter, and it would at least provide some respite from an increasingly chilly conversation.

He turned to the first page of the notebook, and began to read.

1. *The Meeting of Minds*

Christmas comes to Coventry.

It would be too much to hope that it will be white, of course; the only one that this place has to offer is wet and grey. Anyway, a white Christmas would only mean frozen pipes, and ice on the inside of the windows.

There were four weeks or twenty-four shopping days to go when Richard bought the last of his Christmas cards. We are dealing, then, with an organized man. The last card was for his ex-girlfriend, and had been the hardest to choose. When you are actually going out with someone it is easy, you simply get the biggest and most expensive card in the shop, scribble a few florid words and a lot of Xs, stick it in the post, and there you are, the year's work done. But how can a mere card, however tasteful, however well designed, express the complexity of your feelings towards a woman whom you have not seen, properly, for three years, a period almost equal to that for which you were (unofficially) engaged to her?

In the end he settled for one of a snowman pulling a cracker with a rather dissipated-looking reindeer.

How the precinct irked him, at this time of year. Not

because it was too crowded (crowds were comforting) and not because Christmas had become, as any fool could see, a viciously exploitative commercial exercise (for how did it differ, in that respect, from any of society's other festivals or holidays?). It was the atmosphere of enforced enjoyment which was so depressing, which gave rise, all around him, to a palpable mood of suppressed panic and desperation. People couldn't just get away with being unhappy at Christmas. At any other time of year, fair enough, but if they were unhappy at Christmas then they knew, at heart, that they were irredeemably unhappy. Signs of this melancholy truth were on every other face.

I dislike this mode of writing. You pretend to be transcribing your characters' thoughts (by what special gift of insight?) when in fact they are merely your own, thinly disguised. The device is feeble, transparent, and leads to all sorts of grammatical clumsiness. So I shall try to confine myself, in future, to honest (honest!) narrative.

Richard lived in a two-bedroomed flat, on the fourteenth floor of a tower block in the worst part of the city. He shared this flat with a friend, whose name was Miles. They were close friends, with several qualities in common, including laziness and intellectual snobbery. They were both students at the nearby university. ('Nearby'! Sometimes I wonder why I don't chuck this business in altogether and do something useful with my life. For is it likely, we have to ask, that they would be students at a university situated four hundred miles away?) Neither of them had lived in the city for long, or was native to the Midlands. Neither of them was now, or had recently been, involved in a close relationship with a member of the opposite sex.

That evening, after Richard had posted the card to his ex-fiancée, with feelings of such a complicated nature, involving such nuanced shades of ambivalence and contrariety, that it would frankly bore the backside off the pair of us if I were to try describing them, he and Miles had an argument. They were watching the news, and an item came on about Northern Ireland. Some soldier had been blown to bits, or something, or two civilians had been cold-bloodedly slaughtered outside their own homes, or some woman had had to watch while her twin babes were hacked to death by terrorists. The precise nature of the incident is immaterial, as far as this story is concerned. Miles and Richard began to go over the pros and cons of the British military presence, familiar enough ground for both of them. After a while, though, the discussion became acrimonious, and they found themselves disagreeing fundamentally over the nature of the Irish conflict, Miles insisting that it was religious, Richard that it was political. Soon their conversation had ground to a childish stalemate.

'There's no point in my discussing this with you, anyway,' said Richard. 'Let's have a cup of tea.'

'What do you mean, there's no point?' said Miles, following him into the kitchen.

'I mean that it's always the same when we try to talk

about religion. Every time, I come up against the stone wall of your bloody Catholicism.'

'I see. So you think I'm bigoted.'

'Of course not. Look, don't take offence. I don't want to quarrel. It's just that suddenly you become predictable. The whole thing becomes predictable. Suddenly it's not a discussion any more, we're both acting out roles. I know what I can and can't say to you, and whenever you say something, I have to ask myself, Is that what he really thinks, or just what he's told he has to think?'

Back in the sitting room, Miles was subdued.

'I didn't know you felt that strongly about it.'

'It's not *you*, Miles. It's these wretched compromises we have to go through, every day of our lives. We never arrive at the truth, because we're always too busy making allowances. You end up never speaking your mind, you just say what you know the other person wants to hear. You frame a different truth for every context. You can't talk about socialism with a group of conservatives, and you can't talk about conservatism with a group of socialists. If you want to talk about religion, you'll find yourself saying completely different things depending on whether it's a Buddhist, a Christian or an atheist you're discussing it with. If you ask an academic for an opinion, it'll be an academic one, if you ask a doctor, it'll be medical, if you ask a solicitor, it'll be legal. The minute we become socially active, we sacrifice honesty, integrity and neutrality to the impulse to avoid confrontation.' He sighed and concluded: 'It's very depressing.'

'You sound like a friend of mine,' said Miles.

'Really?'

'Yes. I've got a friend who thinks just like that.'

'What's his name?'

'Karen. Haven't you ever heard me talk about Karen?'

'The name's vaguely familiar.'

'She's always complaining that she can never have a proper discussion with anyone.' He thought for a moment. 'You two really ought to get together.'

After a few more minutes, this became a serious suggestion. Richard was opposed to the idea of actually meeting Miles's friend, however. He claimed that the sort of conversation which he envisaged could only be truly impartial, truly detached, if the participants were to remain at a distance from one another. He proposed an exchange of letters.

'All right,' said Miles. 'I'll call her up now.'

Soon afterwards he returned with the news that Karen had responded enthusiastically to the proposal.

'She asked you to write the first letter,' he said, 'and wants to know whether you think the United States or the Soviet Union is the more expansionist. She asked you to link your answer to the mood of increased liberalization in Gorbachev's Russia, and to say whether you think this is indicative of a crisis of identity in the communist countries generally. Just to get the ball rolling, really.'

Richard sat up until three that morning, writing his letter. He found the experience uncommonly liberating.

Miles had told him nothing about Karen: all he knew, then, was that she was female, and that she was roughly his own age. Freed from the constraint of having to adjust himself to the known requirements of his addressee, he was able to express himself honestly, fully, as his head and his heart dictated. He did not even know her surname, or have any idea of where his letter would be sent. He simply wrote 'Karen' on the envelope, and left Miles to address and post it.

Three days later, a reply arrived. Richard picked it up from the doormat, sat down at the kitchen table and looked at the envelope. It was postmarked Birmingham. The stamp was a special Christmas issue. His name and address were typed. The envelope was expensive.

Opening the letter, he found ten pages of large, decisive and tidy handwriting. There were many crossings-out, and here and there a whole phrase had been deleted with Tipp-Ex. The letter began with 'Dear Richard', but ended, 'with very best wishes, Yours in anticipation'. (He had given a purely formal 'Yours sincerely'.)

Having taken in these details, Richard began to read in earnest.

Her analysis of recent developments within the Eastern bloc was, he found, both astute and well informed. It was also infused with a militant anti-Americanism which he felt to be rather intimidating. Her thesis was that the price Gorbachev might end up paying for the liberalization of Soviet Russia was, ultimately, its Americanization, the possibility of which she saw as being the apogee of Western capitalist consumerism. Consumerism and expansionism were, she argued, but different sides of the same coin.

To tell the truth, Richard got slightly bored somewhere in the middle of the letter. It suddenly occurred to him that he was probably dealing with a student of political science, and, while he enjoyed political discussion as much as the next man, politics students tended to be the most insufferable people on earth, in his experience. It perked up noticeably towards the end, however, when she began to talk about the impact of mass communications on relations between the superpowers, and on our received models of political relationships generally. He saw a way in which this could be usefully diverted towards a broader argument about the breakdown of traditional forms of communication, with specific reference to the impact this was having on literature. He didn't feel like writing about politics any more, since he suspected that she had the edge over him, on that subject.

His next letter began:

Dear Karen,

Thank you very much for an interesting and thoughtful letter. You cannot believe how pleased I am to have found a correspondent such as yourself; there are times, as I'm sure you know, when you simply can't be candid even (or especially) with your friends, and although I find the intellectual environment at this university stimulating,

I can see that my discussions with you are, in the end,
going to be much more rewarding. Also, I think that the
different cast of our two minds is bound to make for
fruitful argument: I am an English student, whereas
you (I presume – or will you have to correct me?) must
be studying either politics or history. It could have been
so boring, so sterile, if we were both to bring the same
approach to bear on every topic, but I know, I can feel,
that it is not going to be like that.

Karen's reply came by return of post; after which, the
correspondence continued unabated for the next two
weeks. During this time, the following subjects were
covered, with varying degrees of thoroughness: politics
(again); the decline of the welfare state, with particular
reference to the National Health service; sexism, its
origins and effects; religion; astrology; fashion; and
personal relationships. Consequently, Richard was by
now in reasonably sure possession of the following bits
of information: that Karen was a socialist; that she wore
NHS glasses; that she was blonde; that she held no
religious beliefs; that she was Pisces; that she wore
trousers, not skirts, was partial to denim, never used
make-up, and favoured the colours red and blue; and
that she had had two boyfriends, but had not been going
out with anybody now for more than a year.

At this point they found themselves presented with an
unforeseen problem. There were now only ten days to
go until Christmas, and although neither Karen nor

Richard planned to return to their parents' homes just yet (for Karen, it had transpired, was indeed a student, studying Art History at Birmingham University), the onset of the festive season was, nevertheless, beginning to place an obstacle in the way of their correspondence. Owing to the increased volume of mail handled by the post office at this time of year, it was now taking as many as three days for their letters to be delivered. This was, in Richard's view, an intolerable delay; and so he suggested, in a postscript, that – purely as a temporary measure, of course – they should perhaps continue their conversations over the telephone.

Three days later, Karen telephoned him.

What a charming voice she had, to be sure. It had, unless he was much mistaken, a distantly Scottish lilt to it. There was an attractive roughness about the way she pronounced her Rs when using words such as 'structuralism' and 'Derrida' (for they began by discussing literary theory), an appealingly guttural quality to her intonation when she used phrases like 'the auteurist conspiracy' and 'the camera as voyeur' (for they ended by discussing film aesthetics). He wondered whether his own obvious Home Counties accent was annoying her.

'Well, goodbye,' she said, after forty minutes or so.

'Same time tomorrow?' he asked.

'OK. It's been nice talking to you.'

'And to you.'

'Not going home for Christmas just yet, then?' she asked, after an awkward pause.

'No, not just yet.'

'Had many Christmas cards?'

'Not many. And you?'

'No, not many.'

Richard never got many Christmas cards, certainly not as many as he sent out, and he never sent out more than a dozen. So far there was only one card on the mantelpiece, and that was from his next-door neighbours, a small and noisy family with whom he and Miles normally had no contact whatsoever. He didn't even know their names, for the card simply said, 'Happy Christmas – To All at 48, from All at 49'. This year, as last year, he had replied promptly with a card saying, 'Happy Christmas – To All at 49, from All at 48'. Every year, Richard knew, his other next-door neighbours also got a card, directed to All at 47, from All at 49, and so he was never sure whether he, too, should send a card, to All at 47, from All at 48, particularly as he knew that they were invariably swift to return the compliment, with a card to All at 49, from All at 47. (He never did speak to the small, noisy family who lived next door. Some months later, returning home in the early evening, he found their flat swarming with police and ambulancemen. In a concerted suicide, the father had shot his wife, his son, his daughter and finally himself. They left a short note which read, 'Goodbye Cruel World – from All at 49'. The incident had made the headlines and Richard's picture was on the third page of the evening newspaper.)

In fact, Richard found the impersonality of these

exchanges curiously touching and intimate, certainly by comparison with one of the cards he received the next day, a pretentious effort from an old school friend which contained a long-winded and unnecessary photocopied newsletter. He gave this a cursory reading before opening another envelope, which turned out to contain a card from Karen.

It was a big card, with a detail from Monet's *Water Lily Pond* on the front. 'Dear Friend,' it said inside. 'Not very Christmassy, I know, but I thought you might like it all the same. Have a very Happy Christmas. With Love, Karen.'

He showed the card to Miles, who had just joined him at the breakfast table, and said:

'It's funny, we haven't talked about painting at all. I wonder how she knew I was crazy about Monet.'

'I told her.'

It took a while for this to sink in.

'You told her? You mean you've seen her? When?'

'I wrote to her about a week ago. I told her all sorts of things about you.'

Richard threw down his piece of toast in frustration.

'For God's sake, Miles, why did you do that? That spoils the whole thing, it ruins the whole damn . . . exercise. The point was that we weren't supposed to know anything about each other.'

'Well, she asked me.'

Richard stared at him. 'What do you mean, she asked you? When did she ask you?'

'She wrote to me. She wrote me a letter, asking lots of questions about you.'

'She did that?'

Richard pondered this information in a silence broken, for several minutes, only by his friend's sloppy consumption of breakfast cereal.

'So?'

'So what?' asked Miles, looking up.

'So what did you say about me? What does she know?'

'I told her what you do, what you're studying. I told her where you come from. I told her who your favourite writers and composers and painters and pop groups were. I told her what sort of clothes you wear, what you like to eat, what you like to drink. I described your personality. I told her you were a bit pompous, and a bit conceited, and a bit greedy, and a bit arrogant, but that you were basically OK.'

'I see. Fine. So now there isn't a damn thing she doesn't know about me. Thanks a lot.' Another thought struck him. 'Did you tell her what I looked like?'

'No.'

'Oh, good. Well, I appreciate your restraint.'

'I sent her a photograph. You know – the one of you sunbathing, in Capri?'

Richard got up in silence and withdrew to his bedroom. Later in the morning he heard Miles leave the flat. As soon as the front door had closed, he went into Miles's bedroom and began a patient and thorough search for Karen's letter. It had been fairly carefully concealed, among a pile of old lecture notes in a rarely used drawer. The relevant passage, which Richard's eyes found with determined alacrity, was as follows:

Now you must tell me all about this intriguing friend of yours. I've managed to pick up bits and pieces from his letters, but he doesn't give much of himself away. What does he look like? What does he talk like? I bet he's from the south. He strikes me as being a bit full of himself, but nice with it.

You may wonder what all this has got to do with our supposedly strictly intellectual correspondence. To be honest, I didn't think I'd ever find myself getting interested in these details. 'What does it matter,' I thought, 'so long as our minds meet?' But then, inevitably I suppose, I started to get glimpses of the person behind the thoughts, the ideas, the arguments; and a very nice person it seemed too. So I thought, sod it, friendship is more important than some daft academic experiment. So please, do me this favour, Miles. Be Pandarus to my Criseyde; be Pirovitch to my Klara. Just to satisfy my curiosity, that's all.

Richard put the letter away, feeling mildly betrayed and wildly excited. The hours until the next phone call seemed to pass very slowly.

That evening, they discussed the politicization of the plastic arts in the twentieth century, in the wake of those European painters (particularly the Nabis) who had chosen to involve themselves with an increasingly polemical theatre. This conversation lasted for about ten minutes, at which point Karen asked Richard if he was aware that an exhibition currently running at the Ikon Gallery in Birmingham was reported to provide some striking and recent examples of what she liked to describe as 'the politics of composition'.

'Yes,' he said. 'I read about it.'

'It would be nice if we'd both seen it. Then we'd have something more concrete to talk about.'

'Well, I'm free tomorrow.'

'So am I.'

'Let's go tomorrow, then.'

'Separately, of course.'

'Obviously. You go in the morning, and I'll go in the afternoon.'

'I can't make the morning.'

'Oh. Neither can I.'

'Besides,' said Karen, with a touch of hesitation, 'it would really make more sense if we could talk about particular paintings . . . you know, while we were looking at them.'

Richard drew in his breath. 'That's very true,' he said.

They met by the bookstall at two o'clock. There they exchanged broken words – too broken to be recorded here – while their eyes took in the details of each other's faces and bodies. For about half an hour, they looked at the exhibition, their shoulders in nervous proximity, their eyes talking a new language of quick, embarrassed glances, their heads now together, now apart, as they attempted fitfully to interest themselves in discussion of the paintings. The gallery was uncomfortably warm. Outside, they found that a light snow had started to fall, brushing the pavements and the parked cars, settling and melting on the sleeve of Karen's coat, resting, briefly, at the tips of Richard's eyelashes. He took her arm and they threaded through the thin crowd of afternoon shoppers, until they reached the doorway, bordered with tinsel, of a self-service café and snack bar.

They sat at a table for two, and for the first time found themselves unable to speak. It was Karen who managed to break the silence.

'So,' she said, almost laughing. 'We meet at last.'

They reached for each other across the table and held hands. The snow began to thicken. Over the café's speaker system, an orchestral arrangement of 'Once in Royal David's City' became gradually more noticeable.

On the night before Christmas Eve, Richard cooked a Christmas dinner for Karen in his flat on the fourteenth floor of a tower block in snow-swept Coventry. Miles had gone home to his parents that morning, and Karen would be travelling up to Glasgow the next day. They had planned to have a final discussion of the ideology of Christmas, and in particular its pernicious reinforcement of the role of the family as the basic unit of a patriarchal capitalist society, but somehow the subject never seemed to come up. Instead they exchanged presents and argued over the respective merits of apple and cranberry sauce as an accompaniment to turkey.

What they shared, above all else, by now, was an ache of physical desire, a stretched longing which could no longer be borne, like a gorgeous torture. They undressed each other slowly, fumbling with zips, stumbling over buttons, lingering over the unexpected familiarity of flesh never before seen, never before touched, never before kissed. Then their bodies began a long and intricate conversation, tentatively making their different propositions, elaborating upon them, exploring them, turning them over and over, not hesitating to follow the path of any pleasurable digression, and moving, with inexorable logic, towards a sudden resolution of all contradictions.

They lay still, for an hour or more, skin against skin.

'Comfortable, darling?' Richard said, finally.

'Yes,' she said. 'Very.'

He went to fetch the portable television and set it up at the end of the bed.

'Still comfortable, darling?'

'Yes.' Karen was not at all keen on being called 'darling', but she didn't say anything. 'Are you comfortable?'

'Very.'

There was a carol service on the television. The camera tracked over the faces of angelic choirboys and came to rest on the glimmer of electric candles against stained glass. Richard and Karen watched in silence.

'Happy?' she asked, halfway through 'Away in a Manger'.

'Yes. And you?'

Before the programme was over, their eyes had begun to close.

'This explains nothing,' said Ted, barely able to suppress a cavernous yawn.

'No?' said Robin. 'Does it not explain why Aparna and I have never slept together? Does it not explain what seems to you to be a curious self-discipline in this respect?'

'No.' Ted drained his glass; realizing, as he did so, that he had now lost all track of how much he had drunk that evening. 'I would have thought it suggested, if anything, that you should have done.'

'Why?'

'Well, this is meant to be a happy ending, isn't it?'

Robin looked surprised.

'It's all a bit euphemistic, I suppose,' said Ted, 'but I thought this business at the end – I thought it meant they were falling in love.'

'If you want to be picturesque about it, yes.'

'So surely the whole point,' he continued, after a difficult pause, 'is that this Robin person – '

'His name's Richard.'

'Richard, quite. That this Richard person, and this Katharine woman – '

'Karen.'

'Karen, exactly. That these two people, after messing around talking a lot of intellectual rubbish to each other, finally come to their senses and . . . fall in love.'

Robin took a deep breath and explained, in a tone of exaggerated patience:

'It's meant to be implied, Ted, that they lose something along the way.'

And Ted answered: 'I think I'd like to go to bed now, please.'

They drank up and stepped out into a dark hot summer morning. It was a long walk back to Robin's flat, through narrow lamp-lit streets, past black buildings, down pedestrian subways and across the tatty lawns of council estates. Each was preoccupied with his own tired thoughts, and they spoke only once.

'What is it?' Ted asked.

Robin had stopped to stare at a point roughly three-quarters of the way up a block of flats, on the other side of the ring road.

'Aparna,' he said. 'Her light is on.'

Ted followed his gaze.

'You can tell that from here?'

'Yes. I always look up when I come past here at night. Her light is always on.'

'What can she be doing, at this time of night?'

Robin did not answer, and Ted, who could not bring himself to be seriously interested in the question, did not repeat it. Once they had reached the flat, he watched in silence while Robin fetched a torn and faded sleeping bag from under his bed, and laid it on the sofa.

'Will that be all right?'

Ted suppressed a shudder and nodded. He tried to keep from his mind an image of bedtime at home, the double bed, with Katharine sitting up on one side, propped against the pillows, frowning over the last clues to the cryptic crossword, the corner of the duvet turned back in a gesture of welcome, the warm pink light of the bedside lamp, the electric blanket set to 'medium'. Peter next door, sleeping.

'Do you have an alarm clock?' he asked.

'Yes, why?'

Ted explained about his visit to Dr Fowler, and they set the alarm for nine o'clock.

'I could give you a lift onto campus,' he said. 'You could probably do some work there, couldn't you?'

Robin, who was undressed and in bed by now, again said nothing. Ted assumed that he had fallen asleep. But Robin did not fall asleep for some time. He lay awake, listening to the sounds of Ted removing and folding his clothes; struggling to get comfortable; stirring, turning, breathing ever more slowly, ever more evenly. He listened until the silence was almost complete; until almost the only sound was Ted's occasional, drowsy murmur of the word 'Kate'.

*

Robin's alarm failed to wake either of them, and it was

well after midday when they arrived on campus. While Ted went to see Dr Fowler, Robin sat drinking coffee in one of the university's many snack bars; but ten minutes later Ted was back, in a bad temper. His client had gone home for the weekend, leaving a note on his door saying that he would be away until Tuesday. Robin was no longer alone. He had been joined by a grey-haired, bearded, round-shouldered man; tall (about six foot four) but not as imposing as he might have been, owing to a slight stoop, unusual in one of his age (he was thirty-five, according to Robin, although Ted would have guessed that he was older). His teeth, where they were not yellow, were brown, and he never seemed to stop smoking.

'This is Hugh,' said Robin, perfunctorily.

They took little notice of Ted, but continued to sit side by side, reading. Hugh had a bulky library book, and Robin was flicking through a newspaper. It appeared to be agitating him.

'Have you seen this?' he said to Hugh. 'Have you seen what those maniacs are saying?'

Ted hoped that they weren't going to begin a political discussion, and was relieved when Hugh paid no attention; instead, looking up from his book, he had caught sight of two figures on the other side of the café.

'There's Christopher,' he said, 'and Professor Davis.'

Robin looked round sharply, picked up his newspaper and got to his feet.

'Excuse me,' he said, 'I want to read this in private for a moment.'

As he hurried off, Ted turned to Hugh and asked if he could explain this behaviour.

'Professor Davis is head of the English department here. He's meant to be supervising Robin's thesis. They try to avoid each other as much as possible.'

'I see,' said Ted, uncomprehending. 'Are you doing a thesis too?'

'No,' said Hugh. 'I finished mine eight years ago. It was about T. S. Eliot.'

'And what have you been doing since then?'

'This and that.'

He began to read his book.

'I'm an old friend of Robin's,' said Ted. 'We go back several years. Back all the way to Cambridge, in fact. He's probably told you all about me.'

'What did you say your name was?' asked Hugh, looking up again.

'Ted.'

'No, I don't think he's ever mentioned you.'

This suggested to Ted that Robin must have been preserving a mysterious reticence on the subject of his early life. Now he leaned forward and said, in a low voice:

'Tell me – would you say that you and Robin were close friends?'

'Fairly close, yes.'

'Then tell me this: what do you think is the matter with him?'

'The matter? How do you mean?'

'Why do you think this has – happened to him?'

'Happened? What are you talking about?'

Ted could see that he was being stonewalled. Fortunately, four years of selling computer software had, he believed, taught him to understand the psychology of situations such as this. So he asked:

'When was the last time you saw Robin, before today?'

'About two weeks ago, I suppose.'

'Is that usual?'

'Well, it's not *un*usual.'

'Where has he been?'

'Where has he been? How should I know?'

Ted now changed his tone, to one of calm but urgent pronouncement.

'I think Robin is experiencing some sort of mental breakdown.'

Hugh laid down his book, stared at him for a few seconds and laughed hysterically. Then he stopped, as suddenly as he had begun, and resumed his reading.

'So, you don't believe me?' said Ted. 'So, why hasn't he been on campus for weeks? Why isn't he sleeping, or eating, or washing, or shaving? Why does he never leave his flat? Why has he lost so much weight? Why did he try to make an urgent telephone call to me, his oldest and closest friend?'

'Where did you say you knew Robin?' Hugh asked.

'At Cambridge.'

'Well, that was four years ago. Perhaps he's changed since then. To my mind, there's been nothing unusual about him recently. He often disappears for days at a time.

He often forgets to shave. He always smells like that. He's a student. Worse than that, he's a postgraduate student. What incentive is there to keep up appearances?'

Ted could not follow the logic of this argument.

'Robin is studying for his doctorate. That is a respectable profession like any other.'

'Profession my arse,' said Hugh cheerfully. 'Robin will never finish his thesis. Doctorate my fanny. I've seen dozens like him. How long's he been doing it now? Four and a half years. And do you know why he's nowhere near finishing it?'

'Why?'

'Because he hasn't started it yet.'

Professor Davis was now approaching their table. He was thin, bespectacled, and almost bald, and had a habit of staring around him as if looking hopefully for someone who he knew, in his heart, would not be there. His progress towards them was painfully slow; at one point he tripped on the carpet and stumbled against a plastic table. Behind him, Christopher (who seemed to be about Robin's age) was carrying a tray which held two cups of coffee and a macaroon.

'Professor Davis is actually quite a celebrity,' said Hugh. 'You've probably heard of him.'

Ted found it convenient to nod.

'In the academic world he has the reputation of being something of an iconoclast. His new book, *The Failure of Contemporary Literature*, provides a radical and provocative overview of the last twenty years. Critics have hailed it as the logical successor to his earlier book, *Culture in Crisis*, which provided a radical and provocative overview of the previous twenty years. He and I are old friends. We came to the university at exactly the same time.'

'When was that?'

'Sixteen years ago.'

As Ted pondered this information, the professor finally arrived and Hugh rushed to get him a seat, which he sank into, wheezing like an asthmatic. Christopher drew up a fourth chair and put the tray down in the middle of the table.

'So,' said Hugh, after a pause, 'are you well? How are things in the department?'

'Oh, not too bad, not too bad,' said Davis, helping himself to sugar.

His students hung on these words and nodded sagely after he had spoken them. Then there was another silence. When he seemed about to speak again, Hugh and Christopher leaned forward in anticipation.

'The trouble with getting sugar in lumps,' he said, 'is that two is never enough, and three is always too much. Don't you find that?'

He continued sipping his coffee, thoughtfully.

'I see you've got Kronenburg's new book on narrative aesthetics,' said Christopher, picking up Hugh's library book. He turned to Davis. 'You've read this, of course?'

'It looked a bit too German and theoretical to me,' he said, with a benign smile. 'I gave my review copy away to a nephew in Chipping Sodbury.'

Christopher handed the book back to Hugh.

'The older one gets,' said Davis, with his mouth full of cake, 'the less useful critical theory seems.'

'You mean one should go back to texts?' asked Hugh.

'Yes, perhaps. But then, the more one reads them, the less interesting the texts themselves appear to become.'

'This essentially is what you've been arguing in your new book,' said Christopher. 'It's a radical and provocative viewpoint, if I may say so.'

Davis nodded his acquiescence.

'But does this mean,' Hugh asked carelessly, 'the end of literature as we know it?'

'As we know it?'

'As it is taught in our schools and universities.'

'Ah! No, no . . . indeed not. Far from it. In fact I think – ' here there was an almighty pause, far surpassing any that had gone before ' – I think . . .' Suddenly he looked up, the gleam of insight in his eye. The tension in the air was palpable. 'I think I'd like another macaroon.'

Ted took an immediate liking to Professor Davis. He found him entirely free of a trait which was, in his experience, the failing of most academics, that of excessive commitment to his own discipline. Despite the repeated attempts of Hugh and Christopher to involve him in abstruse and specialized discussions, he refused to be drawn, and seemed far more anxious to talk about computers and the nature of Ted's job. He spent some time trying to convince him of the university's suitability as a venue for his employers' next sales conference; and in return, Ted outlined the many advantages, to a man in his position, of a varied and flexible package of word-processor software. Professor Davis was impressed with the labour-saving potential of his programmes, and admitted that he had long been searching for an alternative to the tedious process of correcting his manuscripts by hand. By the time they parted, they had built up a solid respect for one another, and Ted left with a highly satisfied sense of having dealt with a shrewd and very practical businessman.

*

'Professor Davis is a brainless dick,' said Robin, as he sat in the passenger seat of Ted's car. It was late in the afternoon and they were driving back towards Coventry. 'The only radical and provocative thing about him is the number of macaroons he manages to get through in a single day. I don't know what Hugh sees in him.'

'I don't know what you see in Hugh,' Ted answered. 'He's not at all the sort of person you would have chosen as a friend at Cambridge. From what I can gather he does nothing all day but hang around at the university drinking coffee and eating sandwiches.'

'That's what most of my friends do.'

'Why doesn't he get a job?'

'Because there aren't any academic jobs.'

'Then he should look for something else. It's time he started being realistic.'

'If he were to start being realistic it would be disastrous.

He'd realize that life had nothing in store for him any more. He'd probably kill himself.'

Ted snorted. 'Don't be fanciful.'

'Anyway, Hugh's not an isolated case. There are lots of people like him at this university. People who don't belong here any more, but who like it too much to leave. Except that 'like' is the wrong word for this sort of person – it's much too positive – because anyone who likes universities that much really hates life itself.'

'Yes, but surely in a few years' time, if he managed to apply himself, and if he managed to get himself onto some sort of training programme – '

'Someone like Hugh is completely unemployable,' said Robin, 'because his mind has travelled too far along a particular path. There's a certain sort of intelligence he's gifted with, which, partly as a defence mechanism, partly as a form of egocentricity, he's started to believe is the only sort worth having. This has rendered him quite literally unfit for the company of other human beings.' He looked at his watch. 'You can just drop me at the flat if you like. I suppose you'll be wanting to go home.'

'Yes, I had better be getting back.' Ted had surprised himself, in fact, by not having left already. He was aching, after less than two days' absence, to see Katharine and Peter, but at the same time he was nagged by a sense of business unfinished, duties undone. He had been shocked to find Robin so changed, and it was on the basis of this shock that he had slowly begun to contrive an explanation for the peculiarities in his behaviour. Robin had simply forgotten the kind of person he used to be, in the days when he was happy; and so the arrival of an old friend from Cambridge was neither more nor less than a God-given opportunity, sudden and unhoped-for. Continuity with the past, with that former self which he so desperately needed to retrieve, could be re-established; and he, Ted, was the agent through which the link could be made. Not to seize this chance would be an unforgivable dereliction of the obligations of friendship. At the very least it was worth missing his supper for. 'Still, there's no mad rush,' he said. 'What were you going to do, the rest of today?'

'I'm tired,' said Robin. 'I might go to bed.'

'You've only been up a few hours.'

'I might watch the news. See if any more war crimes have been committed by our leaders today.'

'It doesn't do to worry about what's going on in other parts of the world. Leave that to the politicians. What about doing some writing?'

'I'm sick of that. There's no point.' After a while, he added: 'Maybe I'll do some work on the second story. It's still not right, yet.'

'Why don't we go for a walk?' said Ted. 'There must be a park, where we could go for a walk. It's going to be another nice evening. You could bring your story along. You might get some ideas.'

They were approaching the street where Robin lived. Ted parked the car while Robin went to fetch his second notebook, and then they started walking towards Memorial Park.

'It's a lovely evening,' said Ted, undoing his tie. 'You know, I think I could really get to like it round here.'

'This is a fucking stupid idea,' said Robin.

*

It is another warm early summer's evening, and the world seems, to all intents and purposes, to be at peace; so they set off again, these two strange bedfellows, to walk the final stretch of their friendship's path.

Down Albany Road, and up into Spencer Avenue. This should be familiar territory to Ted, he was here only yesterday, but he was preoccupied then, and is preoccupied now, and he feels no glimmer of recognition. As for Robin, his familiarity with this area is like a bad taste in the mouth, it is like a weight around his neck. He longs to leave these pleasant suburban streets, as soon as possible, for as long as possible, but he has no clear plan of how this can be achieved; and his spirit is so tired, he cannot even find it in him to resent Ted for denying him the temporary means of escape.

They walk, in silence, past the deserted playground of an old school, and they head towards the main road. As they wait at the pelican crossing, a curious phenomenon occurs, and their thoughts begin to concentrate, with a sudden rush of purpose and energy, on exactly the same person. And at last, after so much wilful misunderstanding, so much incomprehension, so much distance and difference, their minds meet, after a fashion. They are both

thinking of Katharine. Ted, with a gleam of far-off content-
ment in his eye, is thinking of how pleased she will be to
see him again, how clean and welcoming she will have
made the house in readiness for his return. He is thinking
of the meals she will cook for him, this weekend, and the
wine he will buy to go with the meals, and the love they
will make after drinking the wine. He is thinking of how
pretty she will look; wondering whether she will be wearing
her hair up or down. He is flushed with a new, grateful
awareness of his own good fortune: their mutual good
fortune, in having found one another.

Meanwhile, Robin's thoughts are all of the past. He is
smarting with the recollection of feelings which he has
spent five years trying to suppress; which he thought he
had forgotten, until yesterday, when Ted had arrived, and
he had once again heard her voice over the telephone.
He is remembering his obsession with Katharine, and
wondering whether she ever realized, or ever suspected.
Or perhaps he is simply shutting the certainty out of his
mind, for safety's sake, since it would have been quite
obvious to most people that Katharine had always suspected, and it was only because she had despaired, in the
end, of his ever making his intentions clear, that Ted's
blunt, straightforward proposal had come like a break in
the clouds. And so if Robin had only been a little more
dynamic, a little more decisive, then who knows, she might
have married him, in the fullness of time, and they would
all have lived happily ever after, even Katharine – who is
not, in case you were wondering, going to be allowed a

voice in this story, because it is the story of Robin and Ted, who have both, in their different ways, resolved to keep her out of it. Which is a pity, in a way, because I think you would have preferred Katharine to either of them, had you been allowed to meet her.

They are now approaching the entrance to Memorial Park, and as they pass through this leafy gateway, Ted realizes that the moment cannot be put off any longer: an attempt must be made, for Robin's sake, to plumb the well of shared memory, to remind him of a time when their friendship was fresh and sustaining; to show him that the past, if it lives on in their minds, cannot be irretrievable. So he sits Robin down on a bench, and says:

'Do you remember that day we rode out to Grantchester, the five of us, you, me, Bernie, Oppo and Little Dave, all on our bikes, and how the sun was shining, and how we'd all finished our exams, and how we stopped at the Red Lion, on the way there, and the Green Dragon, on the way back, and the Black Horse, where we had lunch, and I had scampi, and we all drank champagne, and the sun was blazing away, in the sky, and we sat in the garden, by the river, near the bridge, close to the jetty, just by the boats, and the garden was full of people, young people, like you and me, full of hope, full of fun, full of the joys of spring, except that it was summer, which probably explains why it was raining, for a while, but not for long, and we went inside, and Bernie was drunk, and Oppo was pissed, and Little Dave was completely rat-arsed, and the whole thing was like a scene out of *Brideshead Revisited*.'

But Robin's memory of this incident is slightly different; for he remembers only a drizzly May afternoon, when his examinations, far from being finished, were at their height, and being dragged away from his desk, where he was revising, with an energy born of panic rather than enthusiasm, the works of August Strindberg and Anton Chekhov, and being plonked on a bicycle by Ted in the company of three perfect strangers, the whole charade apparently deriving from the belief that he needed 'taking out of himself'. The ride was long, the day was cold, the pub was full, the benches were wet, the champagne was flat. Nevertheless Robin, too, had managed to get drunk, and the consequence of this had been that he was unable to concentrate on his revision that night and had got an extremely low mark on a paper which should have been among his best.

And so Ted, somewhat taken aback by the discrepancy in their recollection, tries again, by saying:

'Do you remember those long talks we used to have, long into the night, sometimes with a whole crowd of us, talking about all sorts of things, swapping ideas, having arguments, putting the world to rights, talking about politics, and books, and life, and art, and sometimes just with the two of us, drinking coffee, bursting with so much to say that we'd talk until – well, after bedtime, sometimes, about art, and life, and books, and politics, idealistic maybe, but everybody is idealistic at that age, we grow out of it, as time goes by, optimistic maybe, but young people are often optimistic, you get over it, after a while. Do you remember how we used to talk, just the two of us, long into the night, like a scene out of *The Glittering Prizes*?'

But Robin's memory of these evenings contains several material points of contradiction, and falls into two distinct halves: he remembers evenings when there were several people in his room, several of his own friends – scattered, now, and all out of touch – and they would be trying to have a serious discussion about the merits of a particular book, or the integrity of a particular philosophic system, or the trustworthiness of a particular politician, and then at some point or other Ted would barge in, lowering the tone, ruining the atmosphere, forcing the conversation around to his own range of interests, which was not extensive, even then. And the other situation was when Robin would just be preparing for bed, possibly quite early in case there was some work he wanted to start first thing in the morning, and then Ted would arrive, proffering two weak cups of instant coffee as an excuse for entering his bedroom, and he would sit on the bed, and talk about his life, which was not much of a life, even at that stage. And sometimes, in the course of talking about his life, he would talk about his feelings for Katharine, and Robin, who had his own feelings for Katharine which were not, in the last analysis, radically dissimilar to Ted's, would become upset, inwardly, and would not be able to sleep, so that the whole of his next day's work would be ruined.

But Ted, not to be put off by one or two minor inconsistencies in these separate versions of the same event, is soon at it again, saying:

'Do you remember that lovely day, in that last lovely summer, when we went out on the river, the three of us, you, Katharine, and me? Katharine and I had only just got engaged – it can only have been a day or two earlier that I asked her the question that made her mine for ever. We were so much in love. You were standing up, punting, and we were sitting down, watching you. How privileged we felt. Not just privileged to be there, life's chosen young things, in our white suits and summer dresses, eating strawberries, and cucumber sandwiches, and cream cakes, and drinking champagne, but privileged to be with each other, and to be with you. Yes, the two of us felt privileged to be with you, Robin, to feel that we had a friend in you, a shared friend. You bound us together in those days, it was almost like having a child. Of course, now we have Peter. But I have to know, Robin, I need to know now – did you sense any of that at the time? Did you know how much you meant to us?'

But it is Robin's quiet suspicion that Ted is kidding himself, for he remembers the day in question distinctly, and it is not at all as Ted had described it. Ted and Katharine had not arrived at any kind of understanding, of that he is quite certain, because their behaviour together would surely have given it away, and then Robin would not have spent the entire afternoon in an agony of indecision, an ecstasy of trepidation, a stupor of half-formed words and held-back propositions. It is clear that Ted, seduced by the memory of an afternoon which might indeed have appeared romantic to one with his limited sense of the connotations of that word, has projected onto it the over-tones of a situation which had not yet taken shape. Besides, Robin had never been able to punt; nor had Ted for that matter; Katharine was the only one who was any good at punting. So Robin toys with the idea of telling Ted that both of the concepts of privilege invoked in his reminiscence have their flaws; but something advises him that his breath would be better saved.

And so, slightly (but still not sufficiently) daunted by the number of disparities between their different accounts of the same, supposedly shared, experiences, Ted has a final bash at coaxing his friend into a mood of fond nostalgia, by saying:

'What about that night, that unforgettable night, of the last May Ball? That unforgettable night, many of the details of which, I confess, I've forgotten, but one thing does stick in my mind, namely, that memorable conversation we had, on the bridge over the river, as the piper ushered in the dawn. That memorable conversation, the actual substance of which, admittedly, escapes my memory, except that I know Katharine was there too, and the three of us were together, watching the mist roll back from the water, watching the revellers in their jackets and ball gowns, revelling away, strolling beside the river, hand in hand, arm in arm, and I know that the three of us must have made a very handsome threesome, or perhaps foursome, for I forget whether you had anybody with you at the time, although presumably you must have done, now I come to think of it. Do you remember that morning, Robin? Do you remember that dawn? The dawn as it now seems, of our new lives, our brighter future?'

But this time Robin can scarcely believe his ears, so little resemblance does there appear to be between his and Ted's version of this episode, which he remembers vividly, with a nauseous clarity. He remembers the ball, which he had attended, much against his better judgement, as a favour to a friend, who had been looking for someone to accompany his sister. He remembers this friend's sister, who ditched him after about half an hour, for some other bloke, leaving him to wander around in helpless solitude, wretched with embarrassment. He remembers coming across Ted and Katharine, beneath an archway, she with her back against the wall, he with his arms astride her, the frightened look in her eyes as she saw Robin approach, her mouth still wet from the kiss. And he remembers being on the bridge with them, only a few hours later, after they had all had far too much to eat and drink, and Ted was leaning queasily over the muddied waters of the Cam.

'There there,' Katharine had said, stroking his back, slowly. 'There there.'

'No,' Robin now says, five years later. 'No, I don't remember that at all.'

*

Their dialogue was interrupted, at this point, by the abrupt arrival of a plastic football which landed in Ted's lap. A small boy of about three or four came running up, and held out his hands. Ted laughed, offered the ball teasingly, withdrew it, offered it, withdrew it again and then gave it back. The boy failed to see the joke.

'Well,' said Ted, 'that was a very big kick for such a little boy, wasn't it?'

Robin looked away in disgust. He noticed that the boy's father was staring at them. He could not be certain, but he felt that he had seen this man somewhere before.

'Come on, Jack!' he called, and the boy ran off.

Ted was still smiling, but his smile froze when he saw the look of wooden indifference on Robin's face.

'What's the matter?' he said. 'Don't you like children?'

'Not in the way that you do.'

As soon as Robin had said this, Ted assumed such a peculiar expression, so suddenly suspicious and uneasy, that he hastened to add:

'I mean, not to the same extent.' He blundered on, 'I suppose the big difference comes when you have a child of your own, but – I don't see that happening, to me . . . For a while.'

'No,' said Ted. 'Nor do I.'

Ted began to feel the imminence of a number of disagreeable emotions: anger, at the frustration of his efforts at reminiscence; distaste, at what he had seen, over the last twenty-four hours, of Robin's way of life; despair, at the thought of his immediate future; and fear, when he contemplated the differences which lay between them, the murky, unspoken impulses which set Robin apart and which may even have led him to his present impasse. He decided to leave, there and then, before these emotions became too oppressive. It would look odd, but he was under no obligation to behave tactfully. In half an hour he could be back on the M1, heading towards Surrey, and home.

'Look, Robin, I think I'd better be getting along,' he said.

'OK.'

'If you want to stay here for a while, I can find my own way back to the car.'

'Fine.'

Ted waited in vain for a gesture, a look, a point of contact.

'Well, it's been nice seeing you,' he said. 'After all these years.'

Robin smiled.

Ted began to walk away, down the path which leads from the memorial. Turning at the gateway, he gazed at Robin for the last time. He saw a figure huddled, on a warm summer's evening, at one end of a park bench. Briefly it crossed his mind to wonder what on earth he might be thinking. Then he shook his head and made for the road.

Robin was thinking: 'Forces would seem to be conspiring against me.'

PART TWO

The Lucky Man

Friday 4th July, 1986

Alun Barnes, LL. B.,
Pardoe & Goddard,
Fourth Floor,
Churchill House,
18 Jeffrey Street,
Coventry.

Mrs E. M. Fitzpatrick,
Frankley, Isham & Waring,
39 Croftwood Road,
Coventry.

2 July 1986

Dear Emma,

Nice to see you at Margaret's 'do' over in Stivichall last Wednesday. I thought she was looking very well. None of us would have believed she was going to get over it so quickly.

I was wondering whether we could get together one of these days and have an informal chat, prior to the second hearing, about Hepburn v. Greene. I think old Mr Hepburn may be about to start making noises about settling out of court, which from both our points of view would be an *extremely good thing, I think. I was wondering, in fact, whether you'd like to revive our little tradition of meeting at Port's on Fridays at lunchtime, just to compare notes?*

Anyway, I shall be there on Friday, and I'll look out for you.

All the best,

Alun

P.S. Apart from anything else, I've acquired some new evidence in the Grant case which I think it might be in your interest to hear about. Do try to come if you can make it.

*

Emma laid the letter down and made a brief effort at being intrigued. The thing was, it was probably just Alun playing games again, and she had enough of that to cope with from her husband at home, at the moment. The sounds of Alison making another pot of coffee from the office kitchen seemed unusually distracting. A couple of weeks ago she would have been intrigued, no doubt about it: not that the case itself presented any special features of interest, apart from the fact that she rather liked her client, but her appetite for work had been stronger then. Now she was already beginning to feel sapped.

Alison brought the coffee in and lingered unnecessarily over the pending tray.

'Shit,' Emma thought. 'She feels sorry for me, and now she's going to say something.'

'Anything I can give you a hand with? Things are a bit quiet next door.'

On the point of saying no, Emma hesitated, and then changed course:

'You could file these things away,' she said. 'Thank you.'

It was for the pleasure of watching her work, as much as anything else. Alison had been with them for nearly two years: soon she would be taking her articles. She was a neat, dark-haired, dark-eyed woman, and for some time now Emma had been taking quiet, almost surreptitious enjoyment in the way she moved with a rather diffident grace about the office, the angle of her head as she talked, the lightness and quickness of her fingers as they handled a document or opened an envelope. Sometimes she wondered why they were not better friends. There had been an evening when she had invited Alison back home, Alison and her then boyfriend, some student, and the four of them had had quite a pleasant dinner, around the kitchen table; the wine had been warm and fruity and Mark had been very charming. She recalled, with sudden clarity, the fragments of orange pith which she had seen caught between his teeth as he laughed, over the coffee. But friendship needs more fertile soil than is provided by the merely social occasion, and there remained a barrier between Emma and Alison which Emma, for one, had never been able to define, let alone cross: and now, for all her need, seemed as unlikely a time as any.

'Alison,' she began, none the less.

'Yes?'

Words made a tired effort to rise; then sank.

'Do you fancy,' she ended up saying, 'coming for a drink, Friday lunchtime, at Port's?'

Alison shook her head.

'Friday's out. I've got to go down to Northampton, remember?'

'Oh, of course.'

Emma sipped her coffee and licked the rim of the mug absently. She had forgotten about that.

*

Port's was a basement wine bar in the estate-agent district of the city. On Fridays you always got quite a few legal people in there, as well as the crowd from the building society next door, but it was rarely very full. Emma waited on the doorstep for a while, oddly reluctant to broach that dark interior. The city centre had looked surprisingly gentle and cheerful; she had thought how nice it would have been to spend the lunch hour on a bench in the park, with a few sandwiches and a trashy newspaper. It seemed a long time since she had done anything so unpredictable. Even seeing Alun again seemed predictable. She might have known that it would end up happening, and she supposed that he would probably try the same old tricks.

She let the breeze play on her face for a few more seconds, then turned and went inside.

It was dark and hot, but there was no music playing – that was something. Misspelt notices in chalk advertised the day's bargains in salads and Beaujolais. Emma felt, as she descended the stairs, the absurdity of having worn such high heels – they seemed so noisy and impractical – and found that she was clutching her handbag to her bosom with a fervour which would have made her nervousness obvious had she not checked herself in time. Briefly she wished, very hard, that she was somewhere, anywhere else.

Alun was sitting at a table for two in the corner, his briefcase keeping the second chair occupied. Blue striped shirt, red tie, the same light grey suit. But the moustache had gone; and he looked thinner, considerably thinner, since she had last been with him. Tall, too, when he rose to his feet and smiled his yellow smile of welcome at her.

'Emma. You look charming. You are charming. I'm charmed. Please sit down.'

For a dreadful moment she thought that he had been going to kiss her cheek; but they shook hands instead.

'What's it to be? What will you have?'

She asked for white wine and soda. Then they made small talk for about ten minutes.

'Look, Alun, time's getting on,' she said, finally. 'What's all this about Hepburn?'

'Well, he's come to his senses, basically. I've managed to disillusion him about what he might have come out with in the way of a court settlement. These people, they read in the papers about people being compensated to the tune of tens of thousands of pounds. I told him that he wasn't even certain to win, if it came to that.' He smiled. 'Well, I've saved you some work, haven't I?'

'Yes, you have. Thank you. I'm very grateful. Not that things are especially busy just now, as it happens.'

'Oh? Business isn't slackening off, I hope?'

'No, but you know how it is: sometimes you get quiet phases. I'm not complaining, I mean it's nice to have a bit of space. Two people both doing demanding jobs . . . it can be a strain.'

'Two people?'

'Mark and I.'

'Of course. I did warn you, though. A lawyer and a medic: what a combination.'

'We knew what we were doing.'

Alun fell silent and tried to force a meeting with her eyes, but they were elsewhere. Defeated, he began to rummage inside his briefcase, which contained the papers relating to his current cases and also a thermos flask and an apple. His wife made him a packed lunch every day but he quite often ended up throwing it away, preferring to go for pub meals with his friends from work. Meanwhile Emma was thinking of an evening several weeks back, with her and Mark lying side by side and wakeful; she was looking at herself as she lay in that dark and silent bedroom, thinking how stupid it was that she didn't even feel that she could raise the question of a child any more, and if it was all going to come to an end, which she had started to see as a possibility, at last, then had she really missed her chance, a woman of thirty-four, would she be able to find anyone else quickly enough, someone she liked enough, would she even feel like going through the whole rigmarole again? She had felt so lonely that night, sharing a bed in the dark with a man whose bed she had shared for the last eight years of her life, and she felt lonely now, sharing a drink and a bowl of salad with a man whom she had never, it seemed, had much grounds for liking.

'Let's talk about Grant,' he said, and pushed his salad to one side in order to make room on their needlessly small table (there were other, bigger ones free) for a small red notebook.

'Fine,' she said, genuinely relieved. 'What was it you wanted to show me?'

'You've met this chap, have you?'

'Robin? Yes, twice.'

She noticed a flicker of surprise at the fact that she had instinctively used his Christian name.

'Twice?'

'Yes. We met socially, last week.'

He left a short, mannish, tiresomely eloquent pause.

'Well, that's your business. You must know what you're doing.'

'It's not like that at all. We met through a mutual friend. A former client.'

Alun waited, banking on a further explanation.

'Some years ago – I don't know if you remember – I defended this man called Fairchild. Hugh Fairchild. He was being prosecuted by the DHSS for fraud. He'd finished his Ph.D., and he was doing a bit of teaching at the university, earning about ten pounds a week or something, only at the same time he was claiming the dole. So the DHSS finally cottoned on to this and they asked for everything back. It wasn't very much, a few hundred pounds or so, but it was far more than he had, and it actually looked for a while as though he might have been facing some kind of jail sentence. They were cracking down at the time and they seemed to have chosen him as someone to make an example of. So he pleaded guilty of course, and then I got this quite convincing case together and we managed to get him off with a fine and negotiate quite a sensible repayment programme. Which, so far as I know, he's still in the middle of.' She frowned. 'Four years ago, now, at least. Strange how time goes, isn't it?'

'Go on,' said Alun, who disliked it when people became reflective in his company.

'Well, Hugh and Robin know each other, it transpires, so as soon as this thing comes up and he needs a solicitor, Hugh sends him over to me.'

'You've been in contact with Hugh, all this time?'

'Yes, I've had dinner with him. Two or three times. He's a very good cook. He lives in a little bedsitter, out towards Stoke Green. Squalid, but homely. So he had this party out there last week – it was his birthday – and I went along. You know, just to show my face. I suppose I should have guessed that Robin was going to be there, but for some reason it didn't occur to me. I had other things on my mind, at the time. I only spoke to him for a few minutes. Have you met him?'

'Only in court.'

'Well, he was very nervous that morning. As you'd expect.'

'So, what's he like? How would you describe him?'

'Describe him?'

'Yes. I mean, is he the usual child-molester type?'

Emma leaned forward, for the first time, and looked him directly in the eye, also for the first time.

'Let's get this clear, Alun, Robin hasn't done anything. There's no case to answer here. I have absolute faith in him.'

'How can you have faith in someone when you've only spoken to him for a few minutes?'

'We had a long formal interview. I know all that I need to know.'

'So what's going to be the basis of your defence? Character? Are you using a psychiatrist?'

'Of course not. There's no need for that.'

'You see, I have an eyewitness. I would have thought that puts you in a rather weak position.'

'Who – not the boy's father? But he didn't see anything.'

'He saw enough.'

'I've already read his statement. It won't stand up.'

Alun smiled, a quiet, prematurely triumphant smile. He leaned over and picked up Emma's glass, which was empty.

'We've got a lot to discuss. Would you like another?'

'No, thank you, I wouldn't.'

'Want to keep a clear head, I suppose. Something non-alcoholic?'

'No thanks.'

'Well, I'll get you an orange juice. You can always leave it.'

While he was away, Emma picked at the remains of her salad, until she could no longer palate the acrid taste of soft green lettuce leaves. A few questions tumbled through her mind but she couldn't find it in her to follow any of them up. Which was odd, because she knew that only a few months ago this would have been precisely the kind of case which most excited her. She could not remember having felt so listless before, and started to wonder whether perhaps she ought to go and see a doctor: for some days now she had been conscious of a curious heaviness in her head – not headaches, exactly, as she had tried to explain to Mark only last evening, but a sort of throbbing drowsiness which made it hard to concentrate on anything. Well, isn't it nearly that time of the month, he had said, and had seemed to think that he was being sensitive.

'You look tired,' said Alun, lowering the glass gently into her hand. 'Is anything up?'

'It's been a long week. Maybe I'll take the rest of this afternoon off and go home. Or something.'

'Good idea. Put your feet up. You'll feel better for it. Kerry and I are going away soon: two weeks in Portugal. When did you and Mark last have a proper holiday together?'

'Oh, some time ago. Look, the father is your main witness, is he?'

'Yes. His version of events is – well, you've read it

yourself. He says that his son went into the bushes to retrieve this ball and Grant followed him in there.'

'But that's not what happened at all. Robin was there already.'

'So *he* says. But what does a grown man sneak off into a clump of bushes for, at seven in the evening?'

'To relieve himself, of course. Which would explain, wouldn't it, why he was looking "shifty", as I believe the father put it? He'd been drinking tea and coffee all day, with a friend.'

'A friend?'

'A male friend. Parrish. Edward Parrish: they knew each other at university. Have you not been in contact with him?'

'Oh, the elusive Mr Parrish. Yes, I have. I found him very reluctant to testify. He might yet be open to persuasion, though.' Alun crossed and uncrossed his spindly legs, so that they came into embarrassed contact with Emma's beneath the table. 'Well, there we have the facts. There we have the facts which, as you rightly say, are open to quite different interpretations, given their overall sketchiness. And so, since we cannot furnish additional facts, in all probability, we must take the ones which we have already, and arrive at a more *solid* basis of interpretation. Wouldn't you agree?'

'Yes, I suppose so,' said Emma, who was only just beginning to remember how boring he could be. 'What are you suggesting, then?'

'Well, we have the boy's testimony. It's not very coherent,

it's not very conclusive, it just says that this man exposed himself and he was very frightened. Then we have Grant's version, and we have the other's version. Whom do we trust, that's what I'm saying: which of these people is the most trustworthy?'

'I haven't met the father.'

'I saw him a few days ago. He phoned me and said that he'd remembered some more details since making his police statement. As it turned out, they weren't all that significant, but I found out a few more things about *him*. He's going to make a very good witness.'

'Meaning?'

'The man is a pillar of the community. Without a doubt. A scoutmaster, for one thing: good with children. A member of the local RSPCA, for another: kind to animals. He's a staunch churchman, a methodist. He hands out the bibles every Sunday. He started his local neighbourhood watch, he belongs to the Rotary Club, he may even be a Freemason. His wife regularly attends W. I. meetings and is the guiding light behind the Radford Ramblers' and Birdlovers' Coffee Club. They are blood donors, both. What more do I have to say?'

'What does that prove? So he's a family man, and this boy is the only child. All the more reason to be neurotic about his safety. It's an obvious case of overreaction to a harmless and really rather comic incident.'

'I wouldn't try to use that line in your defence if I were you. A man strips naked in front of a terrified child and you call it comic!'

'He did not strip naked. He undid his trousers, that's all.'

'You know, perhaps your trouble with this kind of case, Emma, is that you don't have any children of your own.'

Emma did not know what to say to this. To hide her confusion, she took a sip from the orange juice which she had silently resolved not to touch. She assumed that Alun would apologize, but when he spoke again, his tone remained aggressive.

'So, tell me about Robin. I've just given you a description of a reliable and trustworthy witness. Now tell me what's so special about this man. What gives you so much faith in him after knowing him such a short time?'

Emma swallowed hard; but her voice, once found, was brave, with more of her Edinburgh accent in it than had been noticeable before.

'Well, I found him very likeable, if you must know. Likeable and intelligent: very intelligent. He's depressed, of course. He's going through a bad patch, with his work and everything. It takes a while to get him to come out of himself. But once you've made the effort, it's very rewarding. I thought he was funny, and sharp, and very . . . perceptive.'

Alun left another strategic pause, this one designed to make her feel that he did not think she could possibly have finished.

'Well, OK., Emma,' he said. 'Play it your way. I dare say you've got some tricks up your sleeve which you don't feel like telling us about. Fair enough. But believe me, it's for *your* benefit that I'm asking these questions. I don't want you to get your fingers burned on this one. I want you to be absolutely sure that you know the kind of man you're dealing with.'

'Meaning?'

'Well, for instance.' Alun picked up the red notebook and tapped it with his forefinger. 'You know about Grant's writing, do you? You know that he fancies himself as a writer?'

'Yes.'

'And have you read any of his stuff?'

'No, I didn't think it was necessary. Surely it could have no evidential value.'

'Of course not. But that isn't to say that it wouldn't be illuminating. This notebook was found in the pocket of his jacket on the evening of the crime – I'm sorry, the *alleged* crime. It contains one of his stories.'

Emma took the notebook and flicked through the pages. They were covered with dense, untidy handwriting. She closed the book and read aloud the title which Robin had written in block capitals on the cover.

'*The Lucky Man*,' she said. 'What's so special about it? What's it about?'

'I wouldn't like to give it away. Let's just say that it projects a rather unusual personality,' said Alun, and added, 'You've hardly touched your drink. Is it worth me getting you another?'

'I don't want another. I didn't want that one.'

Emma stood up. She suddenly felt an absolute lack of

curiosity about the contents of the notebook, indeed about the truth behind the case itself. Instead she had a mind to drive out to Warwick and sit in the grounds of the castle for a few hours.

'The point is,' said Alun, draining the last of his lager, 'that you should really persuade him to plead guilty.'

Emma laughed.

'Nice try, Alun. But we're neither of us going to give up.'

'Perhaps there are things he hasn't been telling you. You see, Grant is quite well known around these parts.'

'Well known? What do you mean?'

'This was what the father came to tell me. He'd seen Grant before, but couldn't remember where. That's why it wasn't in his first statement. Apparently every Saturday this man takes his family to play bowls, on the green near the Broadway. The child goes too. And Grant has been bothering them before, it transpires. Watching them. He'd had his eye on that kid for some time.'

Emma stared at him warily.

'I don't believe that,' she said.

'Please yourself. We could both save ourselves a little bit of work again, that's all.'

He followed her up the stairs, and the absurd clicking of her heels against the wooden steps irritated her more than ever. Someone had told her once that it was the kind of noise that men find sexy: perhaps it had even been Mark. She made as little fuss as possible about shaking his hand, which was slippery with sweat, and as she walked away she had no awareness at all of what her parting words had been. The sunshine and the glass of wine were making her sleepy and dizzy.

July 1986: the first week of that month was extraordinarily hot. The tarmac on the pavements was sticky. Sunlight bounced back off the windscreens of shiny new cars, driven by sales reps in their shirtsleeves as they made the last calls of the week. The crowds of unemployed teenagers hanging around in the doorways of shops in the precinct were sporting pale greens and blues this year. Emma walked quickly to the multi-storey car park and cursed herself for having chosen to park out on the roof: the steering wheel was too hot to hold. She opened all the windows, turned the radio on, found her ticket and was pleased to discover that her purse contained enough change. Then, trusting her initial impulse even though it was already rather faded, she drove over to Warwick. The rush of air through the open windows and the cheerful, sentimental music put her in a better mood.

*

Emma is lying by the river on a hot Friday afternoon. She has not bought anything for her husband's supper, in fact she cannot even remember whether he will be in for supper tonight. She used to like her husband, they used to have plenty of things to say to one another. Now each considers the other slightly too selfish for comfort. Nothing has actually been articulated yet, nothing she can put her finger on: there is merely a certain coldness at the breakfast table, a certain tiredness about their lovemaking, an almost too obvious effort to be made when it comes to taking an interest in each other's work. One television programme too many gets watched last thing at night. But this is all, so far. The shouting, the sulks, the suspicion, the blunt recriminations, the unexpected fear – these are treats which life still holds in store for Emma. This languor that weighs down upon her, this semi-conscious decision to let her mind run in lazy circles, perhaps it is an intimation, perhaps it is a shying-off from the certainty of what is about to happen to her life. In which case she can be forgiven, in all charity, for having forgotten about Robin and his problems; at least until the evening, when it is cooler, and she feels ready to turn to the first page of his story.

2. *The Lucky Man*

In a northern town, a man awakes, pulls back the curtains, and peers at an unfamiliar street.

The man, whose name was Lawrence (I don't intend to keep you in the dark, when it comes to relevant details) then got back into bed and stared at the ceiling for a few minutes; not because it was an especially interesting ceiling, but because he was thinking. He had a headache, which made this process difficult. Gradually, though, he began to piece together fragmented recollections of the previous evening: the journey, the railway station, the drive at breakneck speed through dark and twisted streets. After that, nothing. He could not remember arriving at this house.

A slow smile spread across his face.

Somehow he had managed to undress, or someone had undressed him; probably the latter, since his clothes were folded neatly over the back of an armchair in a corner of the room, and he never folded his clothes before going to bed. He was wearing only his underpants. With sudden energy he swung his legs out of the bed and started to dress. Then he noticed his bag, beside the armchair. He opened it and found that it contained clean clothes, several days' worth. So he put on new underpants, shirt, sweater, trousers and socks, and stepped out onto the landing.

From downstairs he could hear a man's urgent voice conversing quietly on the telephone. He also saw that the bathroom door was open, and he took the opportunity to go to the lavatory and wash his hands and face. By the time he descended the stairs, the voice appeared to have stopped.

He opened a door to his right at the bottom of the stairs and found himself in a small, badly lit but cheerful sitting room. Clothes were being dried on a rack in front of the gas fire and there was a table covered with the remains of breakfast, including half a piece of toast and a mug of tea, still hot. Lawrence noticed that the walls were covered with political posters advertising rallies and marches, and alerting him to the fact that, by purchasing certain brands of coffee and chocolate, he was giving implicit support to corrupt regimes in various far-flung countries, many of which he had never heard of, and many of which he could not pronounce. A young man was sitting by the fire listening to a portable radio which was tuned to Radio 3. He looked up when Lawrence came in and said:

'So you made it? The state you were in last night I thought you'd never wake up. Never.'

He had a Belfast accent.

'Where am I?' asked Lawrence.

'How do you mean, exactly?'

'What town is this?'

'This is Sheffield,' said the man; he seemed slightly surprised by the question. 'Would you like some tea?'

'Yes,' said Lawrence, and added, 'I don't know your name.'

'My name is Paul. I think I owe you an apology.'

He handed Lawrence the tea, which was lukewarm and very strong.

'I wasn't aware of it,' said Lawrence. 'I was about to thank you for putting me up for the night.'

'It was the least we could do,' said Paul. 'A slight case of mistaken identity is what happened, I think. We took you for a party by the name of Docherty. Ultimately, though, you will find that James Joyce is to blame.'

This idea seemed to appeal to Lawrence, who grinned broadly, although in a private way, before saying:

'I look forward to hearing you explain that.'

'It's quite simple really,' said Paul, resuming his seat. 'We had instructions to meet this Docherty fellow off the 10.58 train. We'd never seen him before and had no description to go on, but it had been arranged that he would be carrying a copy of *Ulysses*, by James Joyce. So then you show up carrying a copy of the very same book. It was an easy mistake to make.'

What had actually happened – although Paul and Lawrence, unlike the privileged reader, were never to find it out – was this. Docherty, a terrorist by profession, had been invited by a circle of IRA sympathizers in Sheffield, of which Paul was a prominent member, to come and give an informal lecture on the subject of the Troubles. Slides were planned and coffee and cheese biscuits were to have been served afterwards. Now Docherty, before committing himself to the revolutionary struggle, had once been a railway buffet-car attendant, and he still had a nostalgic liking for British Rail sandwiches, as well as an intimate knowledge of the timetable of the Midlands and Yorkshire services. Consequently, while travelling up to Sheffield, finding that his train contained no refreshment facilities, he decided to pop out to the buffet restaurant at Derby, knowing full well that the train was meant to stop there for seven minutes. How was he to know that the driver, whose video recorder was being repaired that week, was determined to get home in time to see a Channel 4 documentary about organic farming, which featured an interview with his aunt's cousin's next-door neighbour, the manager of a health-food shop in Doncaster? So the train pulled out two minutes early, leaving Docherty dancing with frustration on the platform, and leaving Lawrence, who had intended to get off in Derby, but didn't, having fallen into a deep sleep, which will be explained in the fullness of time (but not before), alone in the compartment with the fatal copy of *Ulysses*. Which, when he was rudely awakened by the ticket inspector, and told to get off at Sheffield, he took with him, with a vague and drowsy idea of handing it in to the lost property office. He was, however, forestalled in this plan by the arrival of Paul and his cronies, who bundled him into their car and whisked him off to an anonymous three-storey terrace before he knew what was happening.

'It was only this morning that I discovered our mistake,' said Paul. 'I took the liberty of looking through your jacket.'

'I would have done the same myself,' said Lawrence.

'You don't seem unduly disconcerted,' Paul now ventured, 'to find yourself in a strange house, with a strange man, in a strange town.'

Lawrence smiled his private smile again, slightly more publicly than before.

'Without wishing to sound blasé,' he said, 'this sort of thing happens to me all the time. My life has been a chain of accidents, and I would have it no other way. I don't suppose there's any more tea?'

Paul set about making a fresh pot, and Lawrence asked him, meanwhile:

'This man Docherty – what was he coming here for, anyway? Why all the secrecy?'

'Well I'm afraid that's a secret. I'd soon find myself in very big trouble if I started telling you that. Let's just say he was coming here to address . . . a political meeting.'

'Oh, politics,' said Lawrence, and Paul noticed the bored intonation which he gave to this word.

'Politics doesn't interest you, I suppose? You wouldn't describe yourself as a political animal?' He handed him a new cup of tea, which was weaker and warmer.

'I'm afraid I find it all rather naive, in the long run,' said Lawrence. 'Thank you. You see, nothing gets changed that way.'

'Well, I'd have to disagree with you there. There's too much defeatism around, that's all. If we all tried a bit harder, if more of us pulled together – well, anyway. I suppose you are a religious man, then, from the sound of you? Now there's naivety for you! Religion, as Marx so rightly said, is the opium of the people.'

'That's very true. I'd go along with that.'

'I see,' said Paul, somewhat put out by the readiness of this concession. 'So, you have no faith in politics, and none in religion? Hmm.' He considered for a moment. 'I take it, then, that you are a materialist? That you take, as the purpose of your life, the acquisition of money, without regard to scruple or morality?'

'Not at all,' said Lawrence. 'Money is the root of all evil.'

'I couldn't agree more. But are you, then, no more than a hedonist? Have you chosen, as the wellspring of your existence, the single-minded and unashamed pursuit of pleasure?'

'Far from it,' said Lawrence. 'The pleasures of the world are as fleeting as a breeze, in my experience.'

'My sentiments exactly,' said Paul. He sat down opposite Lawrence and fixed him with a look of puzzled enquiry. 'So, what is it with you, then? What drives you on? Is it knowledge, is it power, is it love? Are you a sentimentalist, or an existentialist, or an aesthetic pantheist? Or just an alcoholic? What is your system? What are the principles that govern your life?'

'My system is to have no system,' said Lawrence. 'And my principle is to have no principles.'

'That sounds highly unprincipled,' said Paul, 'and deeply unsystematic.'

'You do me an injustice,' said Lawrence. 'I have my beliefs, as coherent as your own, perhaps more so. And I live by them.'

'Very well. Do me the honour of explaining them.'

'Well now: take the situation we are placed in at the moment. Two strangers find themselves talking together in a sitting room in Sheffield. Have political circumstances brought it about? Is it the product of ideology? Only to a certain extent. Is religion of any use to us here? Is it part of a huge providential scheme devised by a benevolent God? I would like to see it proved. No, it seems to me that everything we do is merely determined by chance; or, as I prefer to call it, luck. Our so-called choices, these supposedly responsible decisions – ultimately they have to be made in the context of factors over which we have not the slightest control. Realize this, you see, and you are on the way to understanding life. The man who realizes this is the truly lucky man.'

'That's not a very original philosophy,' said Paul, with a dismissive gesture.

'I never said that it was. And even so, very few people have the courage to take it seriously. It's far too frightening for them.'

'And besides, it hardly helps to explain why you are here, does it?'

'But that's precisely the point. There are no explanations beyond those which consist of chains of cause and effect much too large and complicated ever to be traced. I shall probably never know how I came to be here. All I know is that I meant to visit my sister in Derby, but I fell asleep on the train.'

'So there's your explanation: you were tired, and you fell asleep. What could be more simple?'

'But I wasn't tired. I wasn't tired at all.' Lawrence frowned. 'Perhaps I should phone to let her know where I am. Strange, isn't it, to think that not a living soul, besides you, knows that I am here this morning?'

Paul laughed. 'Ah, but you're wrong again. Just before you came down, I phoned the people in your house, and told them.'

'You phoned Coventry?'

'Yes.'

'Now there we have a classic illustration of my argument. Because, you see, if I had not once had a lover who worked in a newsagent's, you would not have been able to do that.'

'What do you mean?'

'Well, I take it that you got the phone number from the front page of my diary? But I would never have had a diary at all, if this lover did not use to get them free from the shop every January.'

'I see.'

'And, as chance would have it, your plan will have backfired for precisely the same reason. Because if that diary did not have a sentimental value, I would have thrown it away long ago, since it is now a year out of date, and besides, I don't live at that address any more.' He paused for effect, achieved none, and continued: 'So presumably your call met with complete incomprehension.'

'No, not at all. I spoke to a party by the name of Amanda. She knew all about you. She even knew why you had left Coventry.'

Lawrence sat up, truly surprised.

'Amanda? Amanda who?'

'I didn't ask. I thought you'd know. She seemed to be a great friend of yours.'

Now Lawrence was extremely confused by this information, because to the best of his knowledge he had no friend called Amanda, let alone one who lived at his old address. However, I see no reason why you should share in his ignorance.

It is a curious fact that two people can coexist in proximity, perhaps occupying the same work or living environment, and yet have completely different images of one another. For instance, Lawrence would undoubtedly have recognized Amanda if he had seen her. Her face would have been familiar, but only as belonging to one of those many figures whom he did not even know well enough to nod to or smile at in casual greeting. Whereas he was, to her, a constant preoccupation, an obsession, the centrepiece of her mental landscape. The word is 'crush', I am told. Her crush on Lawrence began the minute she clapped eyes on him, only a few weeks after they had both started at the university; but it remained, so far, unsatisfied, owing to a series of misfortunes. She had tried for approximately eight months to fake a chance encounter with Lawrence by hanging around the coffee bar of the Engineering building. This was a complete waste of time because Lawrence had no connection with the Engineering department at all, being a student of social sciences. The fact was that Amanda had once seen him taking a book out of the Engineering section of the library, and, foolishly, had thereby concluded that he was an engineer. Actually he had been taking the book out for a friend, who was ill in bed with a chill, the consequence of having left his raincoat on a bus the previous evening, obliging him to walk home in the rain. Amanda had, in other words, made the mistake of organizing her life around a perfectly reasonable bit of observation and deduction, and had ended up spending an enormous amount of time sitting on her own in unfriendly surroundings waiting for Lawrence to turn up, when in all probability he was sitting alone in a different coffee bar, some two hundred yards away, completely oblivious of her existence.

Eventually, too, another dirty trick was played on her. She made it her business to find out Lawrence's address and one day saw a notice on the accommodation board saying that a room was vacant in his house. She had taken

the room and moved most of her possessions in before
she took the precaution of enquiring, of one of her fellow
tenants, which of the rooms was occupied by Lawrence;
and she was duly informed that Lawrence had moved out,
two weeks earlier, to a flat on campus (which was where
Amanda had been living), and that it was, in fact, his old
room that she was moving into. Which was why, when
Paul phoned the number he had found in Lawrence's diary,
it was Amanda who answered; although her familiarity
with his recent movements must, for the time being,
await further explanation.

'I am puzzled,' Lawrence admitted, 'by what you have
just told me. The name Amanda doesn't ring any bells.'

'I think I've got the name right,' said Paul. 'As I said,
she seemed to know you very well. In fact she sounded
extremely concerned about you. She seemed to think you
were in some kind of trouble.'

'Trouble?'

'The police were mentioned.' He noticed that
Lawrence looked very alarmed at the mention of this
word, and asked, 'You're not . . . you know, on the run
or anything, are you?'

'Not exactly,' said Lawrence, shiftily; and then, with
more assurance: 'No, not at all. I was going to get away
from Coventry for a few days anyway. As I said, I wanted
to visit my sister in Derby. It's just that, as it turns out,
perhaps I picked a good time to go.'

'Oh? Why? Have they got something on you?'

Lawrence felt that the least repayment he could make

for his host's kindness was to give him a full explanation; besides which, it provided him with the chance to put forward further illustrations of his theory to one who was, he somehow suspected, a receptive listener. So he began:

'Well, put it this way, Paul: I have certain proclivities. When I mentioned my lover, for instance, who used to work in a newsagent's, I could have been more specific: it was a man.'

Paul raised neither of his eyebrows at this disclosure, but merely said, 'Oh?'

'Now these proclivities have, recently, led me into what can only be described as bad habits. It has become one of the pleasures of my life to go into toilets, public toilets, men's toilets, and to leave messages, and to receive messages. Messages which sometimes lead to assignations. Assignations which are sometimes of a rather physical nature.'

'Well, you're doing nothing illegal there, so far as I know.'

'There is a problem, though, you see. My twenty-first birthday is not until later this year.'

'I see. So you are in technical breach of our country's somewhat unenlightened legislation in this area.'

'Quite. Now this has never presented problems before, but just this week something happened. An incident. I have to admit that I found it rather disturbing. I was in town, doing a bit of shopping, and I thought I'd pop into one of my regular haunts and see if there was any action going on. Turned out to be very disappointing, actually, so I ended up having to write something myself. And when I came out of the cubicle, there was this policeman standing at the sink, washing his hands, and staring at me in the mirror. He watched me very closely as I left, really studying my face, and then he followed me out. I began to walk faster and headed for one of the shopping streets where there would be more people. Just before I got out of earshot he shouted, "Excuse me, son," and then I broke into a run and dashed into a branch of John Menzies. I must have shaken him off because that was the last I saw of him.'

Lawrence had told his anecdote truthfully, but he was, I'm afraid, unaware of certain details which might have put a different interpretation on it. How was he to know that the policeman in question had been anxious to get a message that afternoon to his greengrocer, telling him that he would be unable to make their usual Thursday darts match, owing to an unexpected shift in the week's duty rota? And that he, Lawrence, bore more than a passing resemblance to this greengrocer's son, whom the policeman had met only once, briefly, in the half-light of the lounge bar of The Hare and Hounds? So that this whole incident derived from a simple misapprehension, and Lawrence had not, as it happened, been the subject of any suspicion at all.

'I can see why this might have unsettled you,' said Paul. 'But it's scarcely a reason for turning fugitive, is it?'

'That was two days ago,' said Lawrence. 'Something happened yesterday which was even worse. I got back to my room on campus and went into the kitchen to make myself a cup of coffee. Then my next-door neighbour comes in and tells me that a policeman has been round asking for me. Asking for me by name. He hadn't said what for, but I think I can guess.'

Once again, however, Lawrence had jumped to a too hasty conclusion, for yesterday's visitor had not been a policeman at all, but a third-year biology student, Kevin Cronin, dressed up as a policeman for the purposes of a Drama Society production of Joe Orton's *Loot*, which was in its last day of rehearsal. Now the part of the policeman in *Loot*, as the drama students among you will know, is very small, and Kevin had taken advantage of one of his long absences from the stage in order to visit Lawrence, for the perfectly innocent reason that, being a keen amateur photographer, he wanted to borrow the key to the students' dark-room, which Lawrence, who was secretary of the Camera Club, kept in his possession.

'So there you are,' said Lawrence. 'Perhaps nothing will come of all this, but it alarms me to hear that this Amanda woman, whoever she is, knows something about it and has been in touch with the police. Perhaps it was her who tipped them off. Perhaps she's conducting some kind of personal crusade against people like me.'

'You have my sympathy,' said Paul. 'We live in a society where even liberal values, hardly the most challenging in the world, are being gradually stifled. However, if I were to make a small observation, it would be that you have invalidated your own theory. It seems to me that you are being persecuted, wrongly, for your sexuality. Now, surely, this is not a question of luck. How are these things determined? Genetically, mainly. And there's also an element of personal choice involved.'

'One's sexuality,' said Lawrence, smiling, 'does indeed exert a massive influence over one's actions. This is as true of the young woman who finds herself pregnant and has to marry, as it is of the Cabinet minister who channels his sadomasochistic impulses into the making of government policy. But I must say that in my own case I had very little choice in the matter. I attribute my homosexuality to the fact that Chelsea were relegated during the season of 1978–9.'

Paul laughed and said, 'That I cannot believe. But I'm sure you intend to explain.'

'Of course,' said Lawrence. 'Puberty, you see, is the crucial period. Many young men have homosexual fantasies and even experiences at this point, especially if they are at a single-sex school; which, incidentally, I was not. Anyway, it was at this sensitive stage that I received my first and only love letter. It was deposited anonymously in this bag which I used to carry my books in. I was very excited and spent some days wondering which of the girls in my class could have sent it. Then one lunchtime I went to a talk given by one of the chaps in the sixth form about this trip he'd made to Africa in the holidays, and when he started writing on the blackboard I was amazed to see it was the same handwriting. The note was from him! I was taken aback at first but then when I thought about all the things he'd said about me in the letter I was still quite flattered. I developed an enormous crush on him and eventually I plucked up the nerve to talk to him about it.'

'And?'

'Well, you see, it turned out that the note wasn't intended for me at all. It was meant for my sister, who was at the same school, only three years above me. She had this very distinctive Chelsea supporter's bag but, like many people who aren't really that interested in football, her allegiance was rather fickle, and when they went down to the second division that season she started supporting Liverpool instead, because they were league champions. Naturally she didn't want the bag any more, so she gave it to me. The next day this unfortunate chap had slipped his love letter into it. I ended up fancying the pants off him for about two terms, and finally had my first sexual encounter with a friend of his in the shower after a cross-country run. And I've never looked back since.' Lawrence smiled again and drank up the last of the tea, including a few leaves. Then he assumed a more worried look. 'This girl Amanda – you didn't tell her where I was, did you?'

'Of course not,' said Paul, and added, casually, 'You'll stay for some lunch, I hope?'

'That would be very pleasant,' said Lawrence. 'And then I really must be getting to Derby.'

'I'll just go out to the shop,' said Paul, 'and get a few things.'

He was lying, of course, but he had a good reason: for Amanda had convinced him, over the telephone, that Lawrence had suicidal tendencies, and he had promised to keep him in the house until she arrived.

And now, I suppose, you will be wanting me to explain how she had come to hold this belief.

The truth is that Lawrence's sister, who was a high-minded sort of woman, worked for the Samaritans; and Lawrence, having failed to obtain any answer from her home telephone number, had called her at work. Amanda had been trailing after him all day as usual, and she was hanging around within earshot of the telephone booth when he spoke the words, 'Hello, is that the Samaritans?': from this, coupled with his troubled demeanour, combined with his rapid flight from campus, she drew an erroneous, though understandable, conclusion.

Lawrence, meanwhile, had dashed back to his room, looking out for policemen on the way, and had thrown some clothes into a bag, pausing only to ask a neighbour if she had any travel-sickness pills he might use (he was prone to travel sickness). No, she had said, but Timothy's room is open, and he has some: he keeps them on top of his bookcase. Now this would have been true, three days before; but since then Timothy had split up with his girlfriend. This had induced a fit of depression which he had attempted to counter, one morning, by rearranging the furniture in his room, a process which involved, among other things, moving his travel-sickness pills to the drawer of his desk, and moving his sleeping pills to the top of his bookcase. Lawrence had swallowed at least four of these before his train arrived at Derby (puzzled at the time, as to why they appeared to be doing nothing for his travel sickness), so it is no wonder that he was still half asleep when Paul and his colleagues met him at Sheffield station.

An hour or so later Paul and Lawrence were sitting down to a fine lunch of toast and cheese when there was a knock at the front door. Paul went to answer it: Lawrence followed him and lingered in the hallway. The callers were two policemen and a woman whom he immediately guessed to be Amanda.

'Is he here?' one of the policemen asked.

'Yes,' said Paul.

'Good work. Now let's have a word with him.'

Lawrence turned and fled up the stairs. The policemen started to clatter after him but Paul told them, 'It's all right, he can't get out that way', and they came back down.

'You fool, that's not what we should be worried about,' said Amanda. 'What about the upstairs windows? Let me go up and talk to him.'

She climbed two flights of stairs and found Lawrence in the topmost room of the house, in the process of opening the window and scrambling out onto the window ledge.

'Come any nearer,' he said, 'and I'll jump. I mean it.'

He was telling the truth, for, if we might undertake a

bit of psychology at this point (it hasn't been the strong point of this story so far, I admit), Lawrence genuinely did not consider his life to be of any value, not even to himself; and if the chain of circumstances which we have been following had obliged him to perform a premature and involuntary suicide, that would have been fine by him. As he stood on that window ledge, poised between Amanda in the bedroom behind him, and Paul and two watchful policemen in the garden beneath, he was half inclined to jump. He could easily have jumped.

What, then, prevented him? Well, he was prevented, as it happened, by the bursting of a water-pipe the previous evening in a house four miles away on the other side of Sheffield. The explanation, had Lawrence ever heard it, would doubtless have pleased him. The house in question was the property of one Norman Lunt, who made his living by teaching maths at the secondary school which stood in the street just opposite the front garden of Paul's home. As a consequence of having had to spend the whole evening mopping up water from his kitchen floor, Mr Lunt was now behind with his marking, and had no less than thirty-four sets of homework to get through during his lunch hour. Finding himself distracted from this task by an extremely noisy and foul-mouthed game of football which was taking place in the playground just outside the staffroom window, he had told the players, in no uncertain terms, to go away and continue their game elsewhere. Thus it was that these six children went to finish off the match at the very edge of the playground, near the road, where they never normally would have thought of playing; so that when one of their number, a promising young inside-right called Peter, took a flying shot at goal from well within his opponents' half (which means that he would probably in any case have been offside), the ball soared straight over the fence, gathering speed and height, and hit Lawrence in the pit of the stomach just as he was about to jump. He was sent reeling backwards and had crashed down onto the bed before he even knew what was happening.

'Are you all right?' Amanda said. 'Are you safe?'

She took him in her arms and held him tight. And Lawrence was shocked, more shocked than he had ever been in his life, by the fervour in her voice, by the depth of feeling which it betrayed, by the warmth and firmness of her arms as they clasped him and rocked him gently. He looked at her face, which was tearful, and wondered who she was and why she seemed to care so much for him. And he wondered, too, how this unexpected development would fit into his theory. He thought and he thought, as she rocked him back and forth, but still he could not decide whether everything he believed had, at a stroke, been disproved, or whether all that it meant was that another decision, perhaps the most important yet, had just been made on his behalf.

Emma's first impulse on finishing the story was to telephone Robin. She was quite convinced that it could not be used against him, but she would like to have had certain questions clarified, there and then: there was something about it which left her uncomfortable, something about its intention, its position, which she did not understand. She could either go to the nearest call box, or she could wait until she got home; the problem with the second of these options, of course, was that Mark would probably listen in to the conversation. In a more lucid, or calmer moment, she would have stopped to consider how odd it was that she felt embarrassed at the thought of her husband listening to her as she made a business call to a client. But now, she did not even pause to reflect on the assumption which must have lain behind this embarrassment: the assumption that her husband would not have liked Robin, would not have liked him at all, had they met.

And so she attempted to phone Robin from a call box on her way back to Coventry; but there was no answer.

Two streets away from home, she parked the car for about ten minutes and sat in the dark, rehearsing her lines in the forthcoming argument. Where have you been? You realize it's after ten. I had to go to Warwick. What for, work? Yes, sort of. I suppose you're angry that I haven't made you any supper. No, I don't expect you to wait on me hand and foot, and besides, I'm quite capable of cooking myself a meal when I need to; it's just nice to have some vague idea of where one's wife is at ten o'clock on a Friday evening, that's all. Well, would you like me to draw you a map of my route, with a complete timetable attached? Look, don't hassle me, Emma, it's been one of those days. Fine, join the club.

Silence.

She felt suddenly frightened to be sitting, alone, in that dark summer street, and when she started the engine again the noise seemed deafening. Then as soon as the house came into view she could see that there was nobody in. She felt relieved, and then immediately wary and cross with herself, because all those hateful suspicions which she had projected onto Mark at once began to seep through the cracks in her own fragile consciousness. Why should he be working late on a Friday night? It was a long time since that had been part of his routine; she had to cast her mind back to his houseman days. Perhaps he had gone to get something to eat from the Chinese round the corner. But the burglar alarm was switched on, the curtains were drawn back, and the whole house, as she paced, like an intruder, from room to darkened room, had a dead and empty feel to it.

She made herself a sandwich, watching her reflection in

the kitchen window, poured herself some milk, and found that she could touch neither. She shivered in the stillness. The fridge was humming quietly, and outside, from several gardens away, she could hear a dog barking.

By the time Emma found herself climbing the stairs, a serious unease had overtaken her. She had the sense of a malevolent presence in her home, a sense of intrusion and watchful hostility; it was more stressful, more threatening even than the experience of lunching with Alun and being bullied by him in that wearying legalistic way. Again she paused at the top of the stairs and listened closely to the nervous hush. Then she went into the bathroom and washed quickly and carelessly. Finally she hesitated before her bedroom door, wondering why it was closed, trying to remember whether she had closed it before leaving for work. She never normally closed the bedroom door before leaving for work.

She opened the door and turned the light on. Immediately Mark sat up in bed and blinked at her, and Emma made the mistake of screaming: only a short, high, quiet little scream, but a scream none the less.

'What the hell's the matter with you?' he said.

She sat down on the very edge of the bed.

'You frightened me. I got frightened, I don't know why. I thought there was somebody in the house.'

'Well there was. Me.'

'Yes, I know. I thought you were out.'

'Out? Where would I be at this time of night?'

He made a bit of a show of sitting up, adjusting his

115

pyjama top, pulling the quilt slightly further over to his side. Emma, who had taken off her shoes as soon as she got in, began to unbutton her skirt.

'I'm sorry, did I wake you?'

'I was nearly asleep, yes.'

'It's a bit early to go to bed, on a Friday.'

'I was tired.'

'Why, has it been a busy day?' It was strange how convenient these ritual questions could be, occasionally, as ways of buying time and building up defences.

'Busy enough.'

Emma waited for him to ask where she had been, but he didn't. She undressed down to her underwear and then put on a dressing gown.

'Aren't you coming to bed?'

'Not yet. I made myself a snack. I thought there might be a film on television.'

'Well,' he said, as she left the room, 'try to be quiet when you come back up.'

But two hours later, when Emma came to bed, Mark was not yet asleep. There had been a film, as it turned out, and it had been quite watchable. As she got into bed beside him, Mark did not move and did not say anything, but she sensed that he was still wakeful, and she allowed her hand to rest gently against his shoulder. When this produced no response she said, 'I'm sorry I was so late getting back tonight.'

He turned over and hugged her.

'That's all right,' he said; but he still did not ask her where she had been, and the moment of reconciliation, which she had been so tensely anticipating, was very transitory.

'Has it been such a bad day?' she asked, wanting to hear him talk.

'Oh, it was OK. I feel I'm fighting a losing battle, though, as usual.'

There was a long pause, during which she could tell that there was something he very badly wanted to say to her. When it came, it was not at all what she had expected.

'I had lunch with Liz today.'

'Liz?'

'Liz Seaton. You know, paediatrics. You met her once.'

'Oh.'

'You don't remember?'

'I don't remember meeting her. I remember the name. You talk about her occasionally.'

'Do I?'

'Yes. Her name seems to crop up. You see her a lot, do you? For lunch, and so on?'

'No, not a lot. Very rarely, in fact.'

'That's funny, then, isn't it?'

'What's funny?'

'Well, it's funny that you should talk about her so much if you hardly ever see her.'

'I don't talk about her that much.'

'Why are you telling me this, anyway? Did anything interesting happen at this lunch?'

'No, it was just a lunch, that's all.'

'So why mention it? Why is this the most pressing thing you have to tell me at one o'clock in the morning when we haven't spoken all day?'

Mark disentangled himself from the embrace, which had become more and more distant, and sat up.

'For God's sake Emma, I was making conversation. I was telling you something about my day, like husbands and wives are supposed to do. That's reasonable, isn't it? I mean, it would even be nice if *you* did it occasionally. Tell me something. Tell me about your day. Where did *you* have lunch?'

'It was nothing special. I took some sandwiches to Memorial Park,' said Emma, after a slightly too obvious hesitation. Fearing the silence which immediately threatened to descend, she explained: 'I wanted to think.'

'Think? What about?'

'Oh, just a case.'

'I see. Anything interesting?'

'Yes. Yes, it is interesting.'

At that particular moment, Emma had never felt less interested in the whole business of Robin and the allegations which surrounded him. And this feeling persisted until the morning, so that she read Ted's letter, which arrived during breakfast, with a tired absence of surprise and disappointment which only a few days earlier would have been unthinkable.

Dear Mrs Fitzpatrick,

I must first of all apologize for my delay in writing this
letter. Rest assured that this has been due, and due only,
to the seriousness with which I have been considering
your request for information.

The news concerning Robin has come to me, as you
can hardly fail to be aware, as a terrible shock. I still
shiver to think that we had been drinking together – that
he had been sitting, worse still, in the passenger seat of
my car – only hours, minutes before he committed this
atrocious deed (though one must remember, of course,
that a man is innocent until proved guilty). Perhaps this
seems ungenerous of me, ungenerous to someone whom
I thought, in naivety, that I knew well: but the explanation
is simple, you see – I have a son of my own.

Almost without realizing it, I think I have already set
out my reasons for declining to testify on Robin's behalf.
(And I should perhaps tell you that I will be making a
similar reply to Mr Barnes, who, as you might possibly
know, is acting for the prosecution.) I feel too closely
implicated in the events of that horrific day; I do not
feel, yet, that I can achieve the necessary detachment.
My wife agrees with me, and I feel sure that you too, as
a woman, will understand.

Finally, if I wish you luck in your conduct of Robin's

*case, I must also express the hope, as a lifelong believer
in honesty and fair play, that justice comes to be done.*

Yours faithfully,

Edward Parrish.

*

By the time of Emma's next visit to Port's, a small revolution
had taken place, beginning with the failure of that embrace
in her bedroom in the small dark hours of the previous
Saturday morning.

Very little had been said, between Mark and herself;
neither of them felt that the subject was yet ready for
discussion. But she knew, now, that he loved another
woman, and she had allowed it to be shown that she knew.
Conversation between them had in fact all but ceased, on
any topic. All week he had been finding excuses for working
late, for eating out at night, and on Wednesday he had not
come home at all. On Thursday evening they had had a
short but conclusive argument: Mark had announced, with
a clear knowledge of the significance of what he was saying,
that he would not be coming to the wedding of Emma's
old college friend Helen at the weekend. She would have
to go on her own.

Meanwhile Emma found, at work, that she was pressing
on with a kind of mechanical energy, and actually getting
things done more quickly than usual; but at the same
time she was aware that she was not bringing sufficient
intelligence, sufficient thoroughness, sufficient engage-

ment to bear on her work. By Friday, she was past caring. She had almost forgotten that she was meant to meet Alun at lunchtime and was nearly a quarter of an hour late. He made his annoyance very obvious.

'If you don't mind me saying so,' he said, pushing towards her the white wine and soda which he had, without asking, already ordered, 'you don't look too good. I'd say you'd been losing out on sleep. Am I right?'

She shrugged her shoulders. 'I wasn't aware of feeling tired.'

'Got a lot on at the moment?'

'No, not much. We've been getting through it all quite steadily.'

'And – ' he shot her an intrusive glance ' – how are things at home?'

'So-so,' she said defiantly.

'I see, you don't want to talk about it. Fair enough. We've got other things to talk about, I suppose. Did you bring the story back?'

'Yes, I've got it here.'

She took the notebook out of her case, and it lay on the table between them. Emma realized that she could remember very little about the story and secretly scanned the first page, like a child about to be tested on the contents of an essay.

'You see what I mean about this, then, do you? You see why it throws a totally new light on the kind of man you're defending?'

'Not really. It's just a story.'

'No it isn't, though. That's precisely what it isn't. For a start, the hero bears a great deal of similarity to Grant himself. The same occupation, the same lifestyle, the same homosexual tendencies.'

'Now wait a moment – '

'Just let me have my say, Emma, let me have my say.' She sipped her drink, shocked by the readiness of his impatience. 'Not only that, but it puts forward a system, a philosophy of life, which many ordinary people would find offensive and irresponsible. The hero of this story abdicates all responsibility for his actions and even for his sexual behaviour. Furthermore he is rewarded for it, since no harm comes to him and he ends up in the arms of a woman who loves him. The police are treated as laughable and no effort is made to argue that one should face up to the consequences of the way in which one treats other people. The story accepts a perverse sexuality as being normal and even goes so far as to celebrate the confusion and unpleasantness which it brings about. On top of that, it projects a cavalier attitude towards terrorism.'

Emma fingered her glass and tried to think hard before speaking.

'There are things about it I don't understand,' she said, 'but I don't think you're giving it a chance. I think it's meant as a bit of a joke.'

She was going to have to try harder than this, she knew.

'Does he strike you as someone who has much to joke about at the moment?' Alun asked.

'Of course he hasn't, at the moment. But I thought this

was written some time ago, wasn't it? Anyway, when I say it's a joke . . . I don't just mean that he's trying to be funny. I mean some of it's serious. Isn't there a bit – about halfway through, where somebody says . . . I mean, there are these two people talking, aren't there? And one of them says – well, I can't quite remember what, it's somewhere in the middle, though . . .'

She began to flick through the notebook, panic having frozen her voice; but Alun took it firmly from her hands.

'Why should we argue about the story, anyway, especially if you can't remember it very well? There's no point in quibbling over details. The point is this – what does it tell us about the person who wrote it? Is it written by a person who seems trustworthy, or attractive, or well balanced, or . . . normal? Are those words you would use about the writer of this story?'

Emma admitted, reluctantly, 'Not the first words, no.'

'Quite. And yet *you* trust him.'

'Yes,' said Emma, 'I do.'

'I don't understand you, sometimes. I really don't.'

'You still want me to get him to plead guilty, don't you?'

'You know the advantages.'

'Yes, I know the advantages.'

'But you won't do it?'

'Don't think you can scare me, Alun. I like to make up my own mind about these things.'

'You mean you haven't made up your mind?'

'I didn't say that.'

And yet she knew that when Alun excused himself and

left after only another five minutes, it was because he had already begun to sense victory. She could not understand why she was starting to give in, why Robin now seemed so unimportant, why she had come so badly out of an argument with a lawyer who she knew (or would have known, until recently) was no match for her. For a while she felt angry with herself; and from within this anger a thought, a forbidden thought, arose and, before she was able to suppress it again, had made itself very clear: she wished that she had never agreed to take Robin's case on, in the first place.

*

A small Anglican church in suburban Birmingham; Saturday morning, getting on for noon; drizzle; the blazing July weather nothing but a memory.

Emma, who did not see Helen nearly as often as she would have liked, had been looking forward to the wedding for some weeks. She had bought a new hat and a new dress especially for the occasion, but as soon as she stepped inside the church (wondering, from the complete absence of people outside the porch, whether she had come to the right one) she realized that she was overdressed. She had forgotten that Helen was not popular with her own family, most of whom now lived in Wales and could not be bothered to make the journey down. As for the groom's relatives, they were a sorry-looking bunch; some were clearly sulking at the fact that they were having to wear suits and ties on a Saturday morning and were looking crumpled and hung-over. So far less than twenty people had turned up. Emma ignored the attentions of the usher and went to sit by the first familiar figure she could see, a great-aunt of Helen's whom she had once met at a birthday party. They said hello to one another but she could tell that the aunt did not remember who she was, and they had no further conversation. At least this way, not knowing anyone, she did not have to apologize for Mark's non-appearance.

As she sat there waiting for Helen to arrive, Emma became aware of increasing depression. Partly, she knew, it was to do with the poverty of the occasion itself. She recognized the pieces the organist was playing, and could tell that Helen had chosen them: subtle, melancholy music which she remembered from their days at law school together. But she was also in a position to catch glimpses of the organist, up and to the right of the choir stalls, and she could see that he was a frail and very old man whose fingers were slipping clumsily on the keys. Emma knew that when the hymn-singing started it would be ragged and thin. Also, there was no escaping it, she could never attend a wedding without being reminded of her own, which had taken place six years before that summer. Helen had been there, too. Emma had felt very smug at the time; yet perhaps her friend had done the smart thing by leaving it so late to get married. She realized, now, that she was going to find it hard to congratulate her.

When she turned to watch Helen come up the aisle, she

found her pale and nervous: but their eyes met and they exchanged a quivering smile.

As the service progressed, she felt her strength slowly leave her. She wished that she had an arm to cling onto, even her husband's. Fortunately the aunt sitting next to her was letting slip the occasional tear, so Emma felt less bad about having to keep dabbing at her eyes with a handkerchief; but finally, just when she thought she was going to make it safely through the entire ceremony, something gave way, and she broke. It was during the last hymn, which happened to have been, once (in the days when she used to go to church), one of her favourites. She liked the tune, apart from anything else, but it had a special significance for her because it had been sung at her wedding, too. Now, after only the first two lines, the rhythm dragging beneath the organist's ancient hands, the notes shrill and unsteady, a terrifying sorrow rose within her:

> Dear Lord and father of mankind
> Forgive our foolish ways

Suddenly she was sobbing loudly, louder than anyone was singing, and then people were turning to look at her, and she sank to her knees, and the aunt was laying a bony hand on her arm; smiling sweetly in wrong-headed sympathy.

*

At the reception, which was held at Helen's parents' house, the first thing Emma said to her old friend was:

'Helen, I'm so sorry. I don't know what happened. I spoiled everything for you.'

'Of course you didn't. Don't be silly.' She was still wearing her wedding dress. 'Look, shall we go away and talk somewhere? I haven't seen you in ages.'

They went out into the garden and threaded their way through those guests who were prepared to put up with the grey skies and the threat of rain. These included the groom, Tony, and a group of his friends.

'Hello, Emma,' he said. 'You're looking good.'

'Thank you.'

'Mark not with you today?'

'No, not today. He couldn't make it.'

Tony kissed his wife, and the two women moved on. As they left, Emma heard one of the group asking, 'Who's Mark?', and Tony answered, 'Her husband.' His friend shook his head, and said, wistfully, 'Lucky man.'

The garden backed on to Edgbaston reservoir, and by passing through a little wicket gate they could get out onto the footpath and sit almost by the water. The ground was very damp, but they didn't mind.

'Emmy,' said Helen, 'tell me what's wrong.'

Emma cried in her friend's arms for a while and then she started to talk.

'Oh Helen, what am I going to do?' she said, when she had told her everything. 'What can I do?'

'Well, what do you feel like doing?'

'I don't know. I hate being with him. I hate being in the house.'

'Have you anywhere else to go?'

'No. I don't know. Home, I suppose.'

'Perhaps you should do that, just for a while. Take a holiday. Can you afford to? Are things very busy at work?'

Emma sat up and began to dry her eyes.

'Not very. There's only really one case that needs much doing on it at the moment.'

'What's that?'

She told her the story of Robin, and explained about how she was being advised to change his plea.

'Well, why don't you? Are you so sure that he didn't do it?'

'I was fairly sure, yes.'

'But look, it would make life so much easier for *him* if he pleaded guilty, wouldn't it? Wouldn't it mean a lighter sentence? Saving the boy from the ordeal of having to go to court, and all that? You can get him to understand, surely. That's what I'd do.'

'Maybe.'

'If you did that, would you be able to take some time off?'

'Probably. A week or so.'

'Then do it, Emma, for heaven's sake. Be selfish for once in your life. When was the last time you were selfish?'

Emma summoned a small, grateful smile, and looked out over the cloudy water of the reservoir as it started to swell with the rising wind. Her mind was already searching for the words with which to break the news to Robin.

PART THREE

The Lovers' Quarrel

Friday 18th April, 1986

Forces would seem to be conspiring against me, Robin had thought, as he sat on the park bench and watched Ted disappear from view.

I have all these theories, all these theories about literature, and I can't for the life of me write them down. I have all these stories, all these stories which by some miracle I do actually manage to get written, and nobody will read them. I spend my evenings traipsing from house to house, distributing leaflets for unilateral disarmament and world peace, and the so-called leader of the so-called free world wakes up one morning and decides to slaughter a few hundred Libyans because he's lost a bit of face. The only person I respect, the only one I feel capable of loving, in this whole city, is so bitter and angry at the way people have treated her that she rounds on me at the slightest provocation. I plan a restful holiday in the Lake District, and wind up stuck in Coventry, playing host to some idiot who claims he used to be a friend of mine at Cambridge.

Actually I don't dislike Ted. The indifference he inspires in me is really rather exhilarating. Five minutes out of his company and already I have almost forgotten what he looks like. Some faces fade the minute they leave the room. And some faces never fade. Never, never. At least – what am I, a man of twenty-six – I assume they never fade. Perhaps when I am forty-six I shall have forgotten, completely forgotten, what she ever looked like. Perhaps Kate and I will pass in the street somewhere or other, Bradford or somewhere, and we shan't even recognize each other. I doubt it, though. I can't see it happening somehow. I hope I don't live to be forty-six, for one thing.

Or anyway, I hope that if I live to be forty-six I will by then have left behind all this stuff, all these ideals, whatever you want to call them, these hopes that I carry around my neck like a sack of potatoes; or failing that, that I will perhaps have made something of them, that it will all have paid off, all this waiting, and I will after all be a famous writer or something, and then one night the lights in some studio will be shining bright in my face, and some television presenter on some late-night chat show will smile at me and say:

'Perhaps you can tell us something about your years in Coventry. Looking back, now, does it not seem that this was a particularly formative time for you, in terms of your writing and the development of your theoretical ideas? Can you tell us something about the so-called "Coventry group", and the form your meetings used to take?'

And I will scratch my head, or rub my nose, or cross my legs, and answer, in a tone of detached reminiscence:

'Well, by and large, our meetings used to take the form of us all sitting around in some tacky coffee bar spouting off about a load of books that none of us had read properly.

We did our best to turn Coventry into a centre of intellectual and cultural debate, but frankly a lot of the time it felt as though we were fighting a losing battle. Naturally we modelled ourselves on the Parisian intelligentsia of the 1920s and 30s, but whereas Jean-Paul Sartre and friends had cafés like The Dôme to meet at, we tended to drink our coffee out of paper cups in the local Burger King, opposite the bus station, or, if we were feeling flush, we'd go to Zuckerman's, a mock-Viennese patisserie just down the precinct from British Home Stores. Anyway, I finally got browned off with the whole business, and effectively I had nothing more to do with them after April 1986.'

'*Who were the main members of the group, at the time?*'

'Well, there was me, of course, and then there was Hugh Fairchild, now one of the world's leading authorities on T. S. Eliot, except that nobody has ever heard of him, and there was Christopher Carter, now one of the most obscure and undistinguished literary theorists in England, if not in Europe, if not even in the civilized world, and there was Colin Smith – how could a man with a name like that fail to achieve eminence? – who would almost certainly have gone on to become an immensely respected poet, critic and man of letters, if it were not for this slight problem he used to have with getting out of bed in the mornings, and if only (one can't help thinking) he had ever bothered to write any of the things he was always going on about writing.'

'*I suppose the university used to play an important part in your collective intellectual life.*'

'Yes, it did. It was where we used to buy our sandwiches.'

'*What would you say were the main characteristics of the group?*'

'Pallor, depression, extreme social gracelessness, malnutrition and sexual inexperience. You must forgive me if I sound bitter about this period of my life. To be honest, I find it hard to imagine what it will be like to look back, in twenty years' time, because I find it hard to imagine what it will be like to be twenty years older than I am now. For I am not a man of forty-six, I am a man of twenty-six, and if I look back twenty years, I see myself only as a tiny wee thing who was always refusing to drink his milk at school, and who refused to hold his mother's hand when we went out walking, and who used to think his big sister was the most wonderful person in the world. I never see my sister now, you see. She lives with her husband in Canada. The occasional letter. And the problem with envisaging the kind of man I will be at the age of forty-six, is that I have no idea, really, no idea at all, of the kind of man I am now. I have absolutely no sense of self, if that makes any sense to you. I feel quite hollow. Seeing Ted under these circumstances was really the last thing I needed, because he seems to have a very clear idea of the kind of person I am, but he is so wide of the mark that it does nothing but confuse me. Nobody really knows who I am, that is the trouble, and I need someone, badly, to tell me who I am. Aparna must be the only one who knows, and she refuses to help. She has always refused to help.'

'*That seems to me a rather defeatist attitude. Why palm the*

134

responsibility off onto other people? If you feel that you've lost direction, then it's time to start asking yourself questions. Remind yourself of what it is that matters to you. Your writing, for example.'

'My writing.'

'Tell me about your writing. What are the distinguishing characteristics of your writing? How would you describe it?'

'Well, since you ask, my writing – are you really interested in all this?'

'Of course. Carry on.'

'My writing falls into two distinct categories. There is my creative writing (not the best word, I know, but I can't think of any other) and my critical writing. Now what distinguishes my creative writing, what it all has in common, what gives it a sort of thematic unity, is that it is all, without exception, unpublished. None of it has ever appeared in any printed form whatever, and none of it has ever attracted even a word of praise or approbation from any agent, editor or publisher's reader. Some of it, on the contrary, has elicited letters of rejection expressed with a fervour which can only be described as religious. And then, even within this category, there is a further distinction to be made, between that which has simply never been published, and that which, moreover, has never been read. For there are some works, perhaps for this very reason the most characteristic, the most typical, the most central to my *oeuvre*, which I have not even been able to get my closest friends to read, and which nobody, to my knowledge, has ever succeeded in wading through, however good their intentions. But to turn to my critical works, they have a slightly different quality to them, and this is that they are all, again without exception, unwritten; that they have, in fact, no existence at all outside the imagination of my supervisor (at his most sanguine), and even he is probably beginning to wonder why I have never shown him any of them. Although it must be remarked, in this context, that my supervisor's failure to display any surprise, let alone displeasure, at the non-appearance of my thesis over the last four and a half years, is nothing short of remarkable, and suggests one of two things: either that he is a man of great patience, and tolerance, or that he doesn't give a toss about me and my work, and at least this way he doesn't have to read any of it. So that as long as the university gets its fees, and he gets his salary, it is a matter of complete indifference all round whether I actually write anything or not. I cannot bring myself to be completely indifferent about it, though. Not completely.'

'*And might it be too much to ask what you have been doing in these four and a half years, when you should have been working?*'

'Oh, a number of things, really, a number of things. I've met some interesting people, and had some interesting conversations. I've sat and thought, about this and that. I'm sorry to be so vague, I just find it hard to be positive about the tangibility of my achievements at the moment. Take politics, for instance. A few months ago I would have said I'd matured politically since I'd been here. Now I'm not so sure.'

'*You've suffered some kind of loss of faith, in this respect?*'

'Well, recent events have upset my theories slightly, that's all. I was trying to satirize him at the time, but now I would agree with Lawrence about the naivety of much of what passes for political activity. I don't want to talk about this now, though, it will only make me angry.'

'*But perhaps anger is exactly what you need. Were you by any chance referring to President Reagan's bomb attack on Libya, carried out with the complicity and co-operation of the British government? Is that why you've been hiding in your room like a frightened animal for the last three days, watching every TV programme, listening to every radio bulletin, venturing out only to buy the newspapers?*'

'It's probably not the only reason for the way I feel at the moment, but I have to admit it's upset me more than any other political event I can remember. It terrifies me, the way these people behave. They're barbarians.'

'*The United States was acting in self-defence, within the guidelines of international law. Surely you're not suggesting that terrorists should be allowed to get off scot free?*'

'It's hard to know where to start demolishing that argument, there are so many different ways. The US are claiming justification under Article 51 of the United Nations Charter, but if that is the case, why could they not have gone to the Security Council before taking action (as even Mrs Thatcher did at the time of the Falklands crisis)? Thatcher explained why in Parliament on Tuesday: "Because the Security Council could not have taken any effective action and has not been able to take effective action to deter state-sponsored terrorism". In other words, because it would not have authorized them to do anything. Reagan has ridden roughshod over the legal channels. He knew that an attack on Libya would not constitute self-defence within the terms of Article 51, because the terrorist acts to which he was retaliating could neither be ascribed with certainty to Libya, nor were they sufficiently serious to justify retaliation on the scale which he intended.'

'*But Reagan was responding to two recent attacks, specifically directed at American civilians and servicemen.*'

'Nobody knows for certain whether Libya was behind the TWA bombing. At the moment it seems more likely that it was the work of Abu Nidal's group in Lebanon: they issued a statement on March 26th to the effect that "anything American has from now on become a target for our revolutionaries". Nobody either in America or Britain has yet come clean about the evidence which is supposed to link Libya to this attack. The Commander of NATO, General Bernard Rogers, has merely said, "I can't tell you how we get it, but it's there." Thatcher stonewalled Parliament by repeating that Libya was "demonstrably involved in the conduct and support of terrorist activities". On the 14th, Geoffrey Howe was quoted as saying that there was "solid evidence" of Libyan involvement; later in the day Whitehall sources changed "solid" to "quite convincing". Possibly the source of their information was the monitoring of communications in Cyprus, where Libyan messages could have been intercepted, but this is pure supposition because the government has consistently refused to lay any real evidence before Parliament, for reasons of "security". In any case, five Americans were killed in the TWA bombing, and one other died in the attack on a discotheque in West Berlin on April 5th. To avenge these deaths, Reagan mounted an attack which killed at least one hundred people (according to the most modest estimates) including Gadaffi's adopted daughter. Many of those most seriously injured were Italians, Greeks and Yugoslavs, and the French, Austrian and Finnish embassies in Libya were all devastated. And yet in October 1983, more than 250 US military personnel died in the bombing of the Marine base in Beirut: five months later, the Americans left Lebanon without doing anything to avenge these deaths. Almost every recent act of air piracy or bombing has been claimed by groups in Beirut, not in Libya, but, as many US diplomats and intelligence officers admit, countries like Iran and Syria are simply too big for America to take on at the moment. So instead Reagan has decided to make a scapegoat of Gadaffi because he is small enough to be crushed without the consequences being too serious. So he gets this hate campaign going against him and comes out with statements like the one he made on the 10th: "We know that this mad dog of the Middle East has a goal of world revolution, a Muslim fundamentalist revolution . . . maybe we are the enemy because, like Mount Everest, we are here." But how can you avenge six deaths by sending in the whole of the US Sixth Fleet, including nineteen cruisers, destroyers and frigates and two gigantic carriers (total 140,000 tonnes) loaded with more than one hundred aircraft including F18 and F14 fighter jets, plus the F111 bombers launched from bases in England?'

'*The TWA and West Berlin bombings were simply the tip of a lethal iceberg. Twenty westerners have been killed recently in attacks at Rome and Vienna airports, which were certainly the work of pro-Libyan (if not actually Libyan) groups.*'

'Yes, but what I can't take is the hypocrisy whereby these deaths attract all the publicity and outrage: because the victims are westerners, the United States feels obliged to make a big noise about it. What about, for example, the hundreds of Palestinians murdered within the last year in the Sabra and Chatila camps by pro-Israeli "terrorists" (if we have to use the word)? Anyway, we haven't yet touched upon the part played by our own government in this little fiasco. Why do we alone, of all the European countries, have to find ourselves implicated in an act which Gorbachev has quite rightly characterized as a "crime of banditry"? How can Thatcher allow aircraft to take off on a mission like this from bases in East Anglia and then turn round and praise the residents for showing "courage" in a situation over which they have no control? And then we have to put up with being *thanked* by Reagan, for God's sake: "Our allies who co-operated in this action" (this is word for word) "especially those who share our common-law heritage, can be proud that they stood for freedom and right, that as free people they have not let themselves be cowed by threats of violence." "Free people" – did you hear that? Were we asked? Did we give permission? In a poll conducted on Tuesday 15th, 71 per cent of British people said they thought that Thatcher was wrong to have let the bases be used (a decision which was taken, incidentally, in accordance with an agreement thirty-five years old, no details of which have ever been published). The same night, two thousand people hold a candlelight vigil in Whitehall to protest against the bombing, and the police arrest 160 of them for "obstruction". With a huge tide of public opinion against them, the government wins an emergency debate on the Libyan issue by a majority of 119. And we are "free", according to President Reagan. We are "free people". Well, I'm sorry, I don't feel free any more. I feel powerless, and frightened, and angry.'

'*Well, perhaps we'd better not talk about politics any more. It seems to be a bit of a sore point with you at the moment.*'

'You could say that, yes.'

'*Is there anything else which you would say is worrying you? Anything more personal? Your continued failure to sustain a relationship with a lover, for example?*'

'Well now, let me see. It's true that my track record in this respect is disappointing – or not so much disappointing, perhaps, as catastrophic. I would say that, taking into account my various dalliances over the last few years and their consistently grisly conclusions, I have reasonable grounds for despair.'

'*How do you explain your inability to cope with romantic involvements with women? Does it have anything to do with an unreciprocated attachment, far in the past, from which you have never really recovered?*'

'Well, maybe I am just making excuses for myself, but it does seem to me that I still spend an inordinate amount of time (considering that it all happened five years ago) thinking about Kate.'

'When you say that it "all happened", what are you referring to, exactly?'

'I'm referring to the fact that nothing happened. That is what happened, five years ago, and I am still kicking myself for it. Which is another reason why seeing Ted was the very last thing I needed, just now.'

'And what was it about Kate that you found so attractive?'

'I don't know how I'm supposed to answer that question. One conceives obsessions and then clings to them: reason doesn't enter into it. She was beautiful and intelligent, for what it's worth, but the world is full of beautiful and intelligent women, many of whom I don't find attractive. I suppose retrospectively I can see that we were very well suited, and it galls me to think I wasn't bright or brave enough to realize this at the time. Like many people, I like carrying around a sense of lost opportunity with me, it gives my life some sort of aesthetic aspect, and it is a good excuse for feeling unhappy when things are not going well. I can say to myself, "If only I had married Kate", and pretend that this is the real problem.'

'Is it not the real problem? You mentioned that you have been involved in other affairs. Are you saying that there was nothing fundamentally wrong with these relationships, except for your own destructive wrong-headedness, your insistence on

continuing to live among the ruins of a shattered romantic obsession?'

'Not at all. That would imply that the blame attached to me, whereas the fault was always with the woman, in each case, invariably. Since I have been at this university, I have been involved with three, or perhaps four, or maybe five, or is it two, different women, and each one has been guilty of the same crime: that of not being Kate. Now if this could have been remedied, everything would have gone swimmingly, I assure you. Meanwhile it seems to be a vicious circle which no woman is capable of breaking. Perhaps I should have an affair with a man.'

'*But there is someone who is capable of breaking it, isn't there? What about Aparna?*'

'There was a time, I admit, when I first came here, when I first met her . . . we seemed to get on so well, everything seemed to be working. I didn't think about Kate then, it's true, even though it was all so recent. I wasn't *happy*, exactly, but excited, very excited. We both were. Now I can't even remember when that feeling started to fade. She became so frustrated, so tired of not being taken seriously, and I was no help to her, then. Today we seem further apart than ever. What have I got to offer somebody like that? I look inside myself and I see this emptiness at the centre, and I don't know how it happened and I don't know what to do about it. It scares me almost to death.'

'*This is called making excuses for yourself. You have a lot to offer her: she needs you as much as you need her. Go and see*

her now, and apologize for what you said yesterday, and every-
thing will be all right.'

'Do you think I should? We didn't really get the chance to talk properly yesterday. It would be nice to talk to her again. I'd like to know what she thought of my story, my third story, my favourite; she usually has something interesting to say about them. Perhaps I should go and call on her tonight, and ask her what she thought. Yes, I could do that now.'

'Excellent. A decision. Things are looking up.'

'In the more immediate term, though, I must go to the lavatory. I must have had about twelve cups of tea today already. No question of waiting until I get back to the flat, I'm afraid; it will have to be done here and now, in broad daylight. Still, there are only those two to see me, and they seem to be fairly absorbed in their game. Furthermore, I can see a discreet clump of rhododendrons, which will suit my purpose perfectly. Excuse me for one moment. This will take no time at all.'

3. *The Lovers' Quarrel*

On a railway line somewhere between Warrington and Crewe, a train comes to an unexplained halt.

It had been sitting there for about a quarter of an hour before any of the passengers started to talk to one another. During that time there had nevertheless been a perceptible increase in the level of noise: the shuffling of feet, the crying of children, the rustle of packets of crisps, the clicking of angry tongues. Then a few isolated remarks:

'Typical, isn't it?'

'All that modern technology, and where does it get you?'

'I wouldn't mind if they just told you what was going on.'

'Thirty-five minutes late we are, already.'

From these unpromising seeds tentative conversations began to grow: nothing special, in most cases, just the occasional anecdote about particularly outrageous delays suffered at the hands of British Rail. The sort of story that everybody seems to have stored up, somewhere.

But at a table for four in one of the non-smoking

carriages, a more interesting discussion was about to take place. On one side were sitting two doctors, eminent consultants from the Midlands, travelling down from a weekend's fishing in Scotland (it was a Sunday evening in late August): handsome, middle-aged, quite kindly looking men. On the other side were sitting two students, who were yet to get acquainted. One of them was called Robert – he came from Surrey and was about to start an MA in English at Birmingham University; the other was called Kathleen – she came from Glasgow and was doing a Ph.D. in biology at Leicester. The review section of the *Sunday Times*, which one of the doctors had been reading, was now lying on one of the tables, and Kathleen's eyes were fixed on the front page. Noticing this, the doctor pushed it towards her, and said:

'You can borrow it if you like.'

She smiled. 'No thanks. I never read newspapers.'

'You seemed to be reading this one.'

'Actually I was just looking at the picture,' she said. It was another big feature about the war – military history dusted down again and spiced up to cater for some bizarre but apparently widespread Sunday-morning appetite – and at the top of the page there was a picture of Field-Marshal Montgomery standing in front of a huge tank. 'I was just thinking of how obscenely phallic those things are. Sometimes I think that war is just another thing men have dreamed up as a way of showing off their erections in public.'

One of the doctors looked shocked and squirmed a little. The other merely smiled knowingly.

'Do I detect a women's libber in our midst?'

Robert looked up from his book, which he had not really been reading.

'That term went out years ago,' he said.

'Women's lib, feminism, call it what you like. The young lady knows what I mean.'

'The thing about women's lib, as far as I'm concerned,' said his friend, 'is that it's all right within limits.'

'Exactly! My sentiments exactly. You've put your finger on it there, you really have.'

Kathleen stared at them in amazement, and Robert said:

'Liberation within limits? That seems to me to be a completely meaningless concept.'

Their expressions were puzzled.

'I mean, you either liberate people or you don't, as far as I can see.'

'Liberate them from what, though?'

'Exactly. I mean, what have women got to be liberated *from*?'

'Oppression,' said Robert.

'Yes, but what do you *mean* by that?'

'A lot of this so-called oppression,' said the other doctor, 'is all in the mind. It's all a lot of nonsense.'

'It would take hours to explain,' said Robert. 'Days. Anyway, why hear it from me? Why not ask a woman?'

They all turned to look at Kathleen.

'Yes, come on, it won't do to keep out of this, you know. You can't let your boyfriend do all the talking for you.'

She leaned forward. 'My boyfriend? My *boyfriend*? My God, I've never set eyes on the man before, I sit next to him on a train, and you assume he's my boyfriend. The assumptions people make. The bloody *assumptions*!'

'I didn't mean to be forward,' the doctor said. 'I just thought . . . well, I don't know what I thought.'

Kathleen sat back again, and her voice took on a more pensive tone.

'No, actually that's quite interesting. Quite revealing, really. This man and I have said nothing to each other on the whole journey – what's your name by the way?' she asked, turning to him.

'Robert.'

'I'm Kathleen. Hello.' They shook hands. 'We haven't exchanged a single word, all evening, and yet you still jumped to the conclusion that we were a couple. So obviously you don't *expect* couples to talk to each other. Obviously your idea of a couple, whatever else it includes, doesn't involve the possibility of two people having any kind of rapport, or any wish to communicate with one another. That's odd, isn't it?'

'Now you're putting words into my mouth, though. After all, supposing you two were . . . you know, together or something . . . well, you can't expect two people to have things to say to each other all the time. There is such a thing as a companionable silence. You shouldn't take things so . . . *literally.* That's the trouble with you feminists, you see the worst in everything, you take everything to extremes.'

'Extremes?'

'"Moderation in all things" has always been my motto.'

'Exactly,' said his friend. 'Moderation in all things. Live by that, and you can't go wrong. It covers the lot: work, play – even politics.'

They sat back and smiled; and as they did so, the train shuddered to a start, and there was a collective sigh of relief throughout the carriage. Some passengers cheered sarcastically.

'Moderation in *all* things?' said Kathleen, so aghast that she ignored the long-awaited resumption of movement. 'Are you saying that a *moderate* amount of truth, or fairness, or justice, or happiness, is enough? You mean as long as people are *moderately* free from the danger of starvation, or the threat of torture, or the possibility of being killed by nuclear weapons, then we should all be happy? That strikes me as being a very strange point of view, actually. A very *extreme* point of view, if I may say so.'

Robert and Kathleen decided to leave the train at Crewe, on the off-chance of catching a faster one coming south on a different line. As they sat drinking coffee in the station café, he said to her:

'I must say I really admired the way you handled those two old fogeys in there. They really deserved it.'

'Oh, they weren't so bad, I thought. In a way they

meant well. There are more harmful sorts of stupidity, after all.'

'I didn't help you out much, did I? I just sort of . . . left you to it.'

'I didn't need helping out,' she said. 'You see, the thing about men is . . . My boyfriend, for instance: now he would have tried to help me out, and he would have blown it. He just would have fudged the issue.'

'Your boyfriend?'

'Well, my ex-boyfriend. It's funny, he used to hate seeing me get into arguments. He always used to be afraid that I'd come out worse from them, but the only ones I ever really lost were when he joined in on my side.' She smiled. 'I'm not bitter about it, his motives were good.' Then a frown. 'At least, I think they were. The trouble with him was, it was always so hard to tell what he was thinking. That wonderful capacity men have for angry unexplained silences. I always used to say that Jim's problem was that you could read him like a book: only it was one of those books where you get stuck on page fifteen and just can't get any further.'

'You mean you feel you never got to understand him at all?'

'There were things . . . areas I never understood. Like – ' She leaned forward earnestly. 'Listen – you're a man, aren't you?'

Robert nodded.

'Have you been out with women?'

He nodded again.

'Well, this is how it seems to me: men – some men, anyway, the ones who've at least got *something* going for them – want their girlfriends to be strong and independent, to be good at getting on with people, to be interesting and lively and resilient. Right? But when it comes down to it, don't they rather *resent* it when these qualities actually express themselves? Don't they feel a bit embarrassed and . . . challenged?'

'Do they? I suppose they do, sometimes. It sounds as if you have something specific in mind, though.'

'As I said, I'm not bitter,' said Kathleen, still smiling; and then repeated, more quietly, to herself, tapping the table with her forefinger. 'No, I'm not. I'm *not*.' She looked at Robert again. 'It just used to piss me off, though, that – once, there was a time, and this is what finally did it – he took me out to meet a couple of his friends, a man and a woman, and I got on really well with this guy, we had a really good evening. Then we get home and he accuses me of flirting – *flirting*, for God's sake, with his best friend. I couldn't understand it. I said, "What's the matter, didn't you *want* us to get on, didn't you want me to talk to him? I thought the whole idea was for us to become friends."'

'What he probably envisaged,' said Robert, drily, 'was friendship within limits. He sounds to me like a believer in moderation in all things.' But he realized that this was an inadequate response, and added, 'And that was what split you up, was it?'

'It turned into one of those petty quarrels. Lovers'

quarrels: boring, sulky things where nothing much gets said. He apologized in the end. Or at least, he told me not to take any notice of him, because he was just being difficult.' She pondered this, and shook her head. 'That was an amazing thing to admit . . .'

Robert said, 'Now if you had been friends, and not lovers, that quarrel wouldn't have happened, because he wouldn't have felt he had any vested interest in you. He wouldn't have felt he had property rights over you.'

'Friends, lovers – what's the difference?'

'Sex, I suppose. I take it you were sleeping together?'

'Yes.'

'Well, there you are. It changes things completely, doesn't it? Sex implies possession.' He finished his coffee, and snapped his plastic spoon in half. 'Take it from me: a friendship without sex would have made all the difference. All the difference.'

The thought had occurred to Kathleen before, of course, but she found it interesting to hear it from someone like Robert, and it increased her initial, tentative liking for him. Their train soon arrived and their conversation meandered over onto other, less demanding topics. But when the time came to part at Birmingham New Street station, they had already established enough intimacy for him to feel able to make a suggestion.

'Look,' he said, 'I have a friend who lives in Leicester. I was going to go and stay with him, the weekend after next. How would it be if I dropped in on you while I was there, for a cup of tea or something?'

And this was indeed what he did, except that he ended up spending most of the weekend with Kathleen, rather than with his friend. On the Sunday evening, she said to him:

'I've got an aunt who lives in Birmingham, who I really ought to go and see, one of these days. The only thing is, I don't think she has the room to put me up. I couldn't stay a couple of nights at your place, could I?'

And so Kathleen came and stayed a whole weekend with Robert, in the house which he shared with two other students, during which time she only went and saw her aunt once (and that was just a few hours before she had to go back to Leicester).

Autumn is a hopeful season for young people and for those of an academic frame of mind: it is the start of a new year, and a much more visible, less arbitrary start than that which is deemed to take place in midwinter. Birmingham, which is a gentle and leafy city (I write this for the benefit of those who have never been there) can look beautiful at this time of year, if you catch it off its guard: copper and silver branches stand out against sharp bright sad blue skies, and pockets of dry leaves are rustled and flapped around the corners of tower blocks and neat red terraces. As a time and a place for starting up a serious friendship with a member of the opposite sex, it cannot be recommended too highly.

Robert and Kathleen had this in their favour, then, and, to give them credit, they made the most of it. An immense fondness grew between them. It was founded on an intelligent liking for one another, an intellectual and spiritual compatibility, combined with a sense of ease and quiet pleasure which each took in the other's physical presence: they enjoyed watching each other do things, prepare cups of tea, chop vegetables, turn the pages of a book, stretch out languidly on a sofa and fall into rest. They enjoyed watching each other sleep. And above all, their friendship had one great strength, which was that no guilt attached to it. Because neither of them felt entirely dependent on the other, Robert would not be racked with anxiety if Kathleen was in a bad mood, Kathleen would not torture herself with selfish remorse if Robert was unhappy, and so on. They faced each other's anxieties and depressions robustly and with thinking sympathy. And sex, of course, that great cause of guilt between miserable couples, that tiny vessel from which we expect to be able to pour so many and such varied medicines – affection, reconciliation, celebration, atonement, gratitude, valediction – was not around, in this case, to cloud the issue; was never there, to fall back on, or to use as the beckoningly simple solution to problems with which it had no real connection.

'So is that your new girlfriend, then?' Robert was asked, by one of his house-mates, on a Sunday evening shortly after seeing Kathleen off at the station.

'No,' he said, 'not really.'

He puzzled over the question in his bed that night. He did not want to use the word 'girlfriend' because it implied claims over Kathleen which he felt he did not have. At

the same time the word 'friend' seemed somehow
insufficient. As he thumbed through a private, mental
thesaurus he came to see that there is no word which can
he used to denote a person for whom one feels a strong
and particular affection which is not also loaded with
romantic connotations. This struck him as being
unsatisfactory. In addition, he began to realize that there
were certain actions and gestures which, though
spontaneous and delightful in themselves, were,
similarly, loaded with associations of a sort which he was
not sure that Kathleen would have thanked him for. For
instance, one morning, on a day when Kathleen was
meant to be visiting him in Birmingham, she telephoned
to say that she was ill with flu and wouldn't be able to
come. Every impulse and instinct within him cried out
to send, by immediate dispatch, a large bunch of flowers
together with a sympathetic message. But supposing she
were to take it the wrong way? Supposing the other
women in her house were to see the flowers and to start
teasing her about it? The thought of embarrassing her, or
of overstepping the unspoken (and hence vague)
boundaries which marked out what was and what was
not permissible between them, was enough to prevent
him from doing anything about it at all. As it was, Kathleen
had spent most of that day lying in bed half expecting
the delivery of a large bunch of flowers together with a
sympathetic message, and had been quietly but
significantly hurt by Robert's ostensible lack of concern.
(She had never, however, been able to admit this to him,

for fear of overstepping those selfsame unspoken boundaries.)

They rarely kissed or embraced: usually only at meeting or parting, or to mark an exchange of gifts. The embraces were always short, but it was never clear who gave the signal to discontinue them; the kisses were always on the cheek, not on the mouth, but it was never clear who made this decision. Robert would think to himself, 'I would not go for her cheek, if she were only to offer her mouth', and Kathleen would think to herself, 'I would offer my mouth, but he is always so quick to make for my cheek.' They treasured these moments, none the less, for all their confusion and hesitancy.

In all the weekends which they spent at each other's houses, they never shared a bed. At Robert's house, Robert would sleep on the sofa, in the sitting room, while Kathleen slept in his bed, and at Kathleen's house, Kathleen would sleep on a camp bed, in the dining room, while Robert slept in her bed. Under this arrangement a good night's sleep was guaranteed for all, and there was no danger of one or the other of them trying any funny business. And yet sometimes Robert, lying awake on his sofa, at three o'clock in the morning, would find himself thinking that it might, after all, be nice to feel Kathleen's body lying warm beside him, to listen to the soft ebb and flow of her breathing, to brush lightly against her arms as she slept. And sometimes Kathleen, lying awake on her camp bed, watching the dawn break, would find herself thinking that there was a sense, perhaps, in which it would be pleasant to have Robert lying next to her, a body to cling gently to in the first silent minutes of sleep, a face to awake to in the grave restful light of a late Sunday morning. They both had these thoughts, undoubtedly; but it did not stop them from feeling, in their hearts, that they were right to behave as they did.

One weekend, after this friendship had been continuing for two or three months, two very close friends of Robert's from Surrey came to stay in Birmingham. They were a young married couple and were visiting relatives in the area. It was arranged that they should meet Robert for a drink on the Saturday night, and naturally he was anxious that Kathleen should come along too. It was a very busy period for her – a whole batch of her thesis had to be written up, word-processed and submitted in time for a departmental deadline on Wednesday morning – but she realized that it meant a great deal to Robert (as well as to herself) that she should meet his friends, so she made a special journey over from Leicester on Saturday evening.

An evening such as this will often resolve into two dialogues: Robert found himself talking mainly to Barbara, while Kathleen became engaged in a long and earnest conversation with his old schoolfriend, Nicholas. This conversation, in fact, proceeded almost uninterrupted, conducted in low and earnest tones, heads together, while Robert and Barbara talked more fitfully, the pauses becoming increasingly prolonged as they slowly exhausted their range of topics for discussion.

It was to bring an end to one of these pauses that Barbara remarked:

'You and Kathleen are obviously very close.'

This was an odd thing to say, given that they had barely spoken to each other all evening, but Robert was pleased nevertheless.

'Yes, we are.'

'How long have you been going out with her, now?'

'Oh, we're not "going out",' he explained, smiling at her naivety. 'We don't sleep together, or do any of those things that couples do.'

'I see,' she said, rather surprised. 'So you're just good friends.'

Robert pondered this phrase.

'What a peculiar expression that is,' he said. 'How dismissive, how reductive. That little word, "just", is so devastating. As if the absence of sex from a relationship leaves it at an altogether more trivial level, floundering. Kathleen and I always think of it as being the other way around. If we see two people doing something together we always ask, "Do you think they're good friends?", and if they don't really seem to be enjoying each other's company the answer is usually, "No, just lovers".'

Barbara laughed. 'I see your point. That's what I meant, you see, when I said you seemed very close. You understand one another. You think the same way.'

'Yes, I suppose we do.'

The conversation then returned to its previous halting, unambitious level, and they discussed Barbara's career prospects, the difficulties of getting about Surrey by public transport, and the possibility of their building an extension to their back bedroom. Most of the time, however, they were silent. Meanwhile Kathleen and Nicholas continued unabated.

It was getting on for midnight as Robert and Kathleen entered upon the last few narrow backstreets leading to his house. A strange silence had established itself between them. Kathleen had made occasional friendly openings which had been met only with monosyllables and sarcasm, and now she was growing fearful of having to go to bed before the thing was explained; also, she needed to talk to Robert about his friend; there were questions which she wanted to ask him. So she said:

'Are you angry with me, for any reason?'

'No. I never get angry with you. You know that.'

This had indeed been true, until now.

'You're very quiet this evening, that's all. I mean, normally, an evening like this, an evening out with friends, we'd be talking about it now, we'd be discussing it.'

'Would we?'

'Yes.'

They walked on a few more paces.

'There doesn't seem to be much to say, if you ask me.'

'Oh, doesn't there?' She stopped and turned to him. 'You never told me about your friend, you never told me about all this stuff he's going through. I mean, that guy really needed to talk to someone. What's the matter with you two, don't you ever talk to each other?'

'I don't see him that often,' said Robert, feebly. 'Anyway, what do you mean? What's he been saying to you?'

'He's been telling me about his depression. Has he not talked to you about that? He's been having to take treatment for it. He's been taking days off work without telling people and – well, it started with his sister dying last year, you must have known about *that*, and then some sort of loss of faith. He'd been going to Quaker meetings . . . He was on the point of killing himself a couple of months ago.'

'What – Nick? Don't be silly. He'd never do a thing like that.'

'He told me, for God's sake. He told me that he went to the very top of this bloody great tower block in south-east London and nearly threw himself off. You mean he never told you?' She shook her head in disbelief. 'Men. Jesus! You can't talk to each other, can you? You're so screwed up.'

Robert began to walk on. Kathleen sighed heavily, ran to catch up with him, and took him by the arm.

'I'm sorry, Robert, I didn't mean that to sound hurtful. You know I don't think of you that way. You know I don't lump you in with everyone else.' He slowed down, but almost imperceptibly. 'I'm sorry we didn't talk much to each other tonight, because I like talking to you, I like talking to you more than to anyone. It's just that . . . I think it was important, for him to have someone listening at last. Perhaps I even managed to cheer him up a bit. Do you think?'

'Oh, I'm sure you did.'

'You are?' She was struck by the uncommon note of certainty in his voice.

'Well, it would cheer any man up, wouldn't it?' Robert said. 'Having a pretty woman flirt with him all evening.'

Kathleen stopped in her tracks, Robert walked on. But after only a few seconds he stopped too, and turned to watch her. She had sat down, on the low wall of a front garden; beneath the amber glow of the street lamp she looked very pale and beautiful. When she clasped her arms together, and her body began to shake, Robert went back to her quickly, in a sudden panic, and sat down beside her and put a hand on her leg.

'Darling, I'm sorry. Look, love, I'm sorry, I was . . . I don't know why I said that. It's just a mood I'm in tonight. I didn't mean it. I was . . .'

' . . . just being difficult,' they said, in unison, slowly.

Robert looked away, remembering.

In point of fact Kathleen had been laughing: sad, spasmodic laughter. She had realized all at once, and was trying to see the funny side.

'Shit,' she said. 'We're lovers. Aren't we? We're lovers, and this is a lovers' quarrel, and what really annoys me is we haven't even done any of the *good* things lovers are supposed to do before they start quarrelling.'

'Is that what's going on?' said Robert.

'Of course it is.' Her laughter grew louder, and more

felt. 'God, how stupid! We must be the first couple in the world to be splitting up before we've even started going out.'

'Splitting up? What do you mean?'

'I mean this is the end, Robert,' said Kathleen, standing, and putting her hands deep into her coat pockets. 'Unless I'm very much mistaken, this is the end.'

'What, you mean – you're chucking me?'

'Yes,' said Kathleen, walking on. 'Yes, I think so.'

His mind was fizzing with confusion. It took him some time to form and phrase his objection, and when it was finally ready, it came out sounding prim and indignant:

'But . . . you can't chuck me. I mean, I'm not your boyfriend!'

Kathleen had disappeared from view – presumably not finding this a very persuasive line of argument – and the silence of the midnight streets was now absolute; even her distant footsteps had quite faded away. Robert assumed that she was heading for his house, so he started to follow: but then, before he had had time to catch up, he broke into a run and took a short cut. He felt it was important to have the sofa ready for when she arrived.

Tuesday 15th July, 1986

Robin did not talk to Aparna about his story for another three months. They saw each other during this time, once a week, perhaps more, and for a while it seemed as though his situation had brought about a great change in her. She had been generous with her sympathy, loyal and giving in her support. Robin was reminded, in fact they were both reminded, of the days when he had first come to the university, the days when he and Aparna were new to one another, and they had struck up what he had felt, at the time, was sure to be a lasting friendship: they had talked and argued and read together, and they had laughed, as Robin had never laughed before. Although it was years since he had heard it, he could still remember Aparna's laughter: a tremendous, rippling peal, gathering strength and momentum, and then ringing on, long after the joke was played out, bubbling to rest at last amid a panting and gasping for breath. Her eyes and her teeth had shone like the moon. She was dazzling. And it had been wonderful, in these last three months, to hear her joke again, to feel the irresistible tug of her humour, even when he knew that she was only doing it to distract him from his worries. It had been wonderful, too, when he could no longer suffer the chill of his own despair, to seek out her warmth, the warmth of her trust: for Aparna, alone among all his friends, had never flagged in her conviction that Robin was innocent.

But it was not only her sympathy for Robin which was making her kind; there was also a more personal hopefulness which he had not expected to see in her again. She was more forthcoming about her work. It transpired that, for the first time in more than a year, she had started writing again. A new idea had begun to take shape, and she believed that she had finally struck upon a line of argument which could not fail to meet with her supervisor's approval. It seemed possible that she might finish her thesis after all, that all her effort would be rewarded, that she would finally prove herself in the eyes of the academic authorities who had persisted in doubting her. Robin was staggered by the amount of energy she continued to devote to this project. She was invariably working when he visited her, and she rarely stopped, by her own account, until three or four in the morning.

One afternoon she allowed him to read everything that she had written so far; and they talked about it, at first in her flat, and then over dinner at a restaurant near the city centre. It began as a more or less serious discussion, with Robin expressing real enthusiasm, tempered with criticism on some points of detail; but gradually the tone of the argument became more playful. Aparna teased him about his intellectual prejudices and soon got him reminiscing about Cambridge: she always liked to hear stories about some of the absurd people he had known there. By the end of the evening they were both moderately drunk and helpless with inexplicable laughter. Robin ended up sleeping on her sitting-room floor and realized, just before falling asleep, that he had actually managed to spend an evening without once thinking of the impending trial.

So it was hardly surprising that he should be drawn to Aparna again, on the day when he received Emma's note. It had simply asked him to call in at the office as soon as possible. He had gone at once, and found a different Emma: nervous, brusque, inarticulate. She set out the advantages of a plea of guilty; she explained how serious it would be if he stood trial and the verdict went against him. She said nothing, this time, about her own faith in his case.

'You don't have to decide yet,' she said. 'Just think about it.'

'But why?' said Robin. 'Why have you changed your mind?'

'I haven't,' she said. 'At least, that's not the point . . .'

She tailed off and he sat in silence for several minutes. Finally she laid a hand on his arm and murmured:

'Robin, I have to get some things ready now. Why don't you go home for a while and think it over?'

Back at the flat, he spent half an hour listening to some classical music on the radio; he tidied his room, folding his clothes and putting socks and soiled underwear into a plastic bag; and he cleared out the box at the bottom of his wardrobe, which contained all his manuscripts. He emptied it out by armfuls into the dustbin outside his back door. He cooked himself some beans on toast and used up his last three tea bags. Then he walked to Aparna's tower block, on the far side of the city.

She opened the door and said, from behind it, without looking to see who the caller was, 'Hello, Robin.' By the time he had stepped into the hall her back was already turned and she was heading for the kitchen. 'I suppose you've come round for some tea,' she said. Robin followed her.

'Yes, that would be nice. Though it's not the only thing I've come round for.'

'Of course not. Tea and sympathy. The Englishman's staple diet.'

He leaned against the kitchen doorway, suddenly wary at the return of a familiar tone. And now for the first time she turned to look at him, having filled the kettle, and he saw into her eyes, which were no longer bright, or questioning, or laughing, but dull and bloodshot, and red from crying. Beneath that, there was a distant anger.

Robin turned and said, 'I'll go and sit in the other room, if you don't mind.'

Aparna said nothing. A few minutes later she joined him in the sitting room, carrying two mugs of tea. It was carelessly made, too strong and over-milked, and the mugs had not been washed properly. She placed them side by side on the low coffee table, and opened the glass door which led out onto her balcony. It was a hot, close afternoon, and there was little hope of making the room cooler this way: the main effect was to let in the cries of truant children at play, far below, on a landscaped playground which comprised two swings, a slide, and some concrete hoops. Aparna stood on the balcony for a while, gazing down on these tiny figures as they acted out their noisy fantasies of violence and conflict. Then she went inside and sat opposite Robin. They drank for a few moments in silence.

'So,' she said at last, the words forming with undisguised effort, 'what brings you here?'

'Nothing. I've come to see you.'

'A social call, Robin? I'm flattered.'

'If I've called at an inconvenient time, I could always go.'

'I wonder if you would. You'd be surprised if I said yes, wouldn't you?'

'Is this an inconvenient time?'

'It would be rude to throw you out straight away, because you probably walked all the way here and you're feeling tired. Besides, I don't mind having you around. You don't take up much space.' All at once she started to drink very rapidly, and had got through most of her mug of thick, brown tea before putting it down in disgust and saying, flatly: 'I'm going to leave this country, one of these days. I'm going to leave it . . . to stew in its own juice.' She smiled a bitter, mischievous smile, and her eyes gleamed briefly.

'So will I.'

'You, Robin? Where would you go?'

'I don't know. Where would you?'

'Home, of course. Back home. You can't do that, though, can you, because this *is* your home. So where would you go?'

'You told me you'd never go home. Hundreds of times you've told me that. Don't tell me you've changed your mind.'

Aparna did not answer him directly, but said:

'England must be a wonderful place to be, for the English. You have so much freedom here, so much opportunity, so much interest, so much variety, such beauty. Why do they want to shut me out of all that?'

'These rose-tinted spectacles you have on today,' said Robin, ' – where can I get a pair?'

'I will start liking you more, Robin,' said Aparna, 'when you wake up to the idea of how privileged you are. How damn lucky you are, in where you were born and in all the chances that have been given to you.'

'We can change places if you like,' said Robin. 'You can stand up in that bloody court in three weeks' time.'

'I'm sorry about that, Robin, you know I am; but you're going to come out of this thing all right, it's obvious. People like you always do. The courts were designed for people like you. For a start you've done the smart thing by choosing a woman lawyer who cares about you. She'll wipe the floor with that man, I can see it happening now.'

'What do you mean, "people like me"?'

'I mean clever, middle-class, well-educated, heterosexual Englishmen. People who've had it their own way for hundreds of years and will continue to do so, till kingdom come.'

They both fell silent; and when Robin finally spoke, it was as if he had just been roused from sleep.

'You can tell me what's happened, if you like,' he said.

She looked at him questioningly, and he elaborated: 'To bring on this sudden burst of anti-imperialism.'

'Sudden?'

Robin picked up an old newspaper which was lying on the table.

'I seem to have caught you in a bad mood,' he said.

'A bad mood.' Aparna repeated the words slowly. 'This is a mood, Robin, which I have been in for two years or more. Or hadn't you noticed?'

'Do you know,' said Robin, 'I just don't feel in the mood for an argument right now. Isn't it funny? I just don't think I could handle it.'

'Then you'd better read your newspaper.'

He put it back on the table.

'Don't tell me: you've been to see your supervisor. You've shown him all the stuff you've been working on for the past six months. And he's raised a sceptical eyebrow, patted you on the head, and asked you out to dinner with him again.'

There was a short silence.

'Those bastards. Those bastards don't realize how much this bloody degree means to me. They've no intention of letting me finish this bloody thing. Nothing would please them more than to see me get on the next plane back to

India, so they'd never have to spend half an hour with me and my work again. That's what they really want.'

'So that's exactly what you're going to do, is it?'

'You've got no right to criticize me, Robin. Six years I've been fighting for this thing – six years out of my life – and I'm not a young woman any more. Not young at all. And the fact is, whatever people try to do to me, I'm still a free agent. I can still choose. I can choose to carry on fighting, or I can *choose* to give in. And that might just be what I do.' Robin said nothing, so she continued: 'Anyway, as it happens, your diagnosis was correct. I have been to see Dr Corbett, and I can report that he conducted himself in his usual fashion. I'm sure he believes that he was perfectly pleasant to me: charming, even. As if I came all those bloody miles to be charmed by some pot-bellied middle-aged academic. He started off by telling me that I was "looking good". Was this a reference to my clothes, my face, my figure? I don't know. Then we chatted about "how I'd been". That was interesting: it transpired that he didn't even know where I'd been living for the last two years. And finally, just to fill up the time, as it were, we talked about my work. We talked about this little thing I've been writing for one-fifth of my bloody life, and which he's made me start again, and rewrite, and start again, and rewrite, and start again, till I've gone blue in the face. And what did he have to say this time, about my one hundred pages, my thirty thousand words, my six months' sitting up here and writing? He found it "interesting"; he thought it had "potential"; but, he said it needed "tidying"; he thought I had been "emotional" and "aggressive", just because I had tried to put down something of what I *feel* about these writers, for God's sake, these *Indian* writers, who somebody has got to rescue from these bloody English critics with their theories and their intellectual imperialism. And then, yes, he said I must come round to supper some time. And somehow, it just came up in the conversation that his wife is in America at the moment, visiting her cousin.' She shook her head. 'You see, intellectually these people are subtle. This disdain, this condescension, it's never articulated. So people don't believe you when you tell them it's there. But I know it's there. I can feel it. I've been trying to squeeze my way past it ever since I got here. Well, maybe it's time to stop.' Her tone changed, became sadder, but no softer. 'God, I miss my parents, Robin. You don't know. Six years. I miss them . . . *so* . . . *much*.' Then she asked: 'Would you be sorry to see me go?'

Robin shrugged. 'I suppose so.'

She smiled her most brittle smile. 'You'd miss your little trinket, would you? Your bit of local colour?'

'That's not how I think of you, actually.'

'I wonder. I think you're all the same, when it comes down to it. The whole lot of you. You let yourself down, didn't you, that day in your flat, when I showed you the book? Wouldn't it make life easier if I just played along with what people want of me? All Corbett wants is for me to be strange and exotic: he'd love it if I walked into there wearing a sari and strumming a sitar. He doesn't want the truth about my country: none of you do. He doesn't want to know that *this* city has an Asian community of its own, and he could find out more about India in an afternoon here than I have any intention of telling him. People like that . . . it's the worst way of using people. They decide what they want you to be, and then they *push* you and *push* you into that mould, until it really hurts. It hurts deeply.'

From the lack of expression in Robin's voice, it was not obvious that he had been listening to any of this.

'Do you mind if we change the subject? I came here to talk about something, and I don't have much time.'

Aparna looked at him sharply, surprised. A flicker of pain shone from her eyes, as if stabbed, but within a second it was gone.

'We can talk about whatever you want, as long as it's of interest to you. Only don't let me stand in the way of your busy schedule.'

'I came to ask if I could have my story back. I'm trying to round up all the copies of the things I've written.'

'Of course. I'll go and get it for you.'

She went into her bedroom and returned very quickly with Robin's notebook.

As he took it from her, he asked, 'What did you think of it?'

'I quite enjoyed it. I quite enjoy all your funny little stories.'

'What does that mean?'

She sat down again and sighed.

'Well now, how important is it to you that I'm honest

about this? What do you fancy today – sweet Aparna or sour Aparna? Do you want her warm, or cold? What's on the menu, Robin?'

'Today,' he said, 'it's very important that you're honest.' Then he reconsidered. 'I say that, but it doesn't really matter. I'll never know, will I, whether you meant it or not? So you can say what you like. Say what you like.'

'Say what I like? That gives me a lot of scope. I hope you mean it.' This sounded almost jocular, compared with her next remark: 'You're a funny man, Robin. A strange man.'

'Why do you say that?' he asked, coldly.

'Well, because you are always making these obstacles for yourself. Always trying to make out that life is harder than it is.'

'You think that things have been pretty easy for me, don't you?'

'Anyone could see that. Anyone but you.'

'What's that got to do with the story, anyway?'

'It has everything to do with it. I mean, love doesn't have to be like that, does it? You know it doesn't. These two people – how is it possible to have any sympathy with them? They should simply have made up their minds one way or the other, and then got on with it.'

'I don't see it as being that simple.'

'Of course you don't. I suppose now you're going to tell me that the same thing happened to you once.'

'Yes, as a matter of fact it did.'

'Poor girl.'

'Who?'

'Whoever it was you messed about like that. She chucked you, did she?'

'Yes, as it happens.'

'Good.'

There was a decisive pause, before Robin stirred in his chair and said, with a touch of irritation:

'What I wanted was your opinion of its literary merit.'

'That's what I've just given you. I can't separate "literary" merit from what a story is *saying*. Why do you think all the academics here hate me so much?'

'Did you find it amusing? Did it make you smile, the irony of it?'

'Not really. What people call irony in literature is usually called pain and misunderstanding and misfortune in real life, and that doesn't make me smile. There's too little love in the world as it is, for me to find it amusing that two people should be incapable of expressing their feelings for one another. It's the same with that horrible story about the lucky man. He was so obviously so stupid, so unthinking about the way life really works, you just wanted the narrator to say something about it, or punish him or something.'

'A lot of people thought that story was funny. You've just lost your sense of humour, over the years.'

'But you can't laugh alone, Robin. Nobody laughs alone. I would laugh, if I had other people to laugh with.'

'Do you remember,' Robin asked, and his voice was quiet with anxiety, 'how you used to laugh with me?'

'I used to laugh with all sorts of people. Perhaps you were one of them.' She did not notice the effect these words had on him, but hurried on: 'These people who found your story funny – they were men, were they?'

'Mostly men, yes.'

'I imagined they would be. You see, men enjoy irony because it is all about feelings of power and detachment and superiority, the things they are born with. Female laughter and male laughter are quite different. I don't think you understand the laughter of women at all: it is all to do with liberation, with letting things out. Even the sound is different, not like that barking you hear when men start laughing together.'

'Are you saying I could never write anything that a woman would find funny?'

'I'm just saying that you shouldn't always be surprised when people don't dance to your tune.'

This provoked another short silence, which Robin showed no inclination to break.

'So,' Aparna continued, 'you think you've been unlucky in love, do you?'

'I've spoiled a few good friendships with women over the last few years, if that's what you mean.'

'They can't have been that good.'

'Well, that's for me to say, isn't it?'

'No, not really, because I don't think you understand the nature of friendship at all. Men usually don't. As soon as they start feeling *real* friendship for a woman then they can't cope with it any more, so they convert it into something romantic. And that's when everything falls apart.'

'You seem very full of answers today.'

'Somebody has to explain these things to you, when you come in here looking like a walking question-mark. Writing all these stories which are just disguised questions, cries for enlightenment. Somebody has to start sorting through all these tangles. My advice to you would be to *learn*. You should learn to spend more time, loving more people, in more ways. Loving someone means helping them, it doesn't mean just . . . dumping your excess emotion into their lap. Your kind of love, it's a self-gratification. *Un*learn it, Robin, before it's too late.' He looked unconvinced, so she added, angrily: 'You certainly won't get anywhere by flirting with homosexuality. It's pathetic, the way you tiptoe round the subject all the time, fascinated, like an uninvited guest peering through the window at a party. Yes? Now come on, Robin, either you knock at the door and walk right on in, or you leave it alone. Why this voyeuristic obsession? Make a decision, for once in your life. But that's not your way, really, is it? You've been taught to toy with subjects, not to involve yourself in them. That wonderful English education, how good it's been at protecting you from the world.' She sighed, rhetorically, and concluded: 'I would give anything to have had an English education.'

'So what should I do?' said Robin: quieter, flatter, more mechanical than ever. 'I should follow your example, should I? See nobody; love nobody; feel nothing. Living alone all this time, looking down on the world in anger from the fourteenth floor.'

'I wouldn't have any regrets about the way I've spent the last two years,' said Aparna, 'if I'd got my work done. If they'd *let* me get my work done. Nothing else really matters. I don't need friends any more, you see; whereas I think you still probably do. These cold, intellectual friendships you cling to. Did you ever notice how all your friends used to dislike me? How suddenly all that brilliant debate, that spontaneous wit, would dry up as soon as I sat at the table, with my serious eyes and my comical earnestness? I bet they still only have to hear my name and they curl up at the edges. Do you ever talk to them about me? Or is the subject of *people* slightly too mundane for your high-flown level of conversation nowadays?'

'Why have you continued to see me, Aparna?' Robin asked. 'I'm puzzled. I'm intrigued. The thing I'd really like to know, before I leave, is why you've continued to see me.'

'I like you,' she said. This made Robin laugh, very briefly and softly. 'And once, we could have helped one another.'

'Once?'

'That time . . . when was it, it must have been last summer. You kept promising me that we would go up to the Lake District together. You had some friend who had just bought a cottage up there, and we were going to go up and spend a week or two. You were going to ring him and ask if we could use it. You kept telling me about all these places you had seen as a child, and how you wanted to go back, and I can remember thinking, to share in something like that . . . it might have been fun. You talked more about your family in those days, didn't you? Now you never talk about them.'

'I associate that area . . . with having a family. It's funny, isn't it? They mean nothing to me now. Such distances. Other things started there too, I think. It was an age I was at. It would have been so nice to go back.'

'Why? What would it have achieved?'

'I don't know. You would have come with me, would you?'

'Of course I would. We could have stood by a lake at sunset, and held hands. It would have been very romantic.'

'Perhaps I should see my parents . . . go and see them. What do you think?'

'Perhaps we are both thwarted romantics, Robin, and it would have been the start of a passionate affair which would have been either the saving or the death of us both. Perhaps I could have swept you off your feet, and made you forget everything. Even the mysterious K.'

'"K"? What do you mean?'

'These sets of lovers you always write about. Always R and K. When are you going to tell me about her, Robin? When are you going to come clean?'

When he did not answer, Aparna slipped back into her tone of fierce reminiscence. 'Anyway. Promises, promises, always promises. You never phoned your friend. We never made it on our sentimental journey, second class. You were toying again, weren't you? I'm not saying you realized it,

178

I'm not saying that you meant to, but you weren't being serious with me. Not really. When *will* you ever be serious about something, Robin? Life for you is just a gloomy irony – and that makes things so easy, doesn't it?'

'I'm serious about my writing.'

'Are you? There are a few serious ideas, I suppose, which you always make a point of slipping in: these little literary hobbies of yours, like suicide.'

'Suicide?'

'Yes. There's always a reference to suicide in your stories. Often quite gratuitous. Like that poor family, in your first story, or the depressed friend, in this one. Nothing ever comes of it. You flirt with the idea, as you do with everything else. Perhaps you're doing it to prove – '

'Look, Aparna, shall I tell you what I came here to tell you? I spoke to Emma today. Emma, my lawyer? She doesn't want to defend me on a plea of not guilty any more. She thinks I did it.'

Aparna lowered her eyes; and her voice, now, was all gentleness, all kindness.

'I'm sorry, Robin. I had no idea, you know I hadn't. Why didn't you tell me earlier? I don't know what to say.'

Robin was hoarse with unhappiness; he could barely speak.

'Could I have another cup of tea, please?'

'Yes, of course.'

She took the two mugs and went into the kitchen; and as she filled the kettle, reached for the tea bags, poured the milk, she bit her lip and tried to find encouraging words, forms of consolation. Perhaps she would ask Robin to stay for the evening, cook him a meal, snap herself out of this vengeful mood. She made the tea as fast as she could, and went to rejoin him. She would sit next to him on the sofa.

But Robin had gone. And the other thing she noticed was that, instead of the childish laughter and shouting, she could hear a confusion of more urgent, adult voices rising from the playground. Not knowing, not guessing, not even fearing, she rushed out onto the balcony, and looked down. Already quite a crowd had gathered around the body.

PART FOUR

The Unlucky Man

Friday 19th December, 1986

It was at last beginning to dawn on Hugh that he would never find an academic job. The realization had made its inroads slowly, like the winter weather, and he had developed the same way of coping with both, namely lying in bed for as long as possible, with the gas fire turned up to top heat. Half the time he would doze, half the time he would be wide awake, staring frog-eyed at the ceiling, his hand resting absently on his genitals. In this position, in order to avoid thinking of the future, he would think of the past. He would rehearse the proudest episodes of his life and compare them with his present state of stifled inertia: his graduation; his six-month tour of Italy and the Greek islands; the flush of intellectual excitement in which he had completed his MA thesis; his first sexual conquest; his second sexual conquest; his last sexual conquest; the publication of his note on line 25 of 'Little Gidding' in a 1976 issue of *Notes and Queries*; the second graduation ceremony, at which he had been awarded his doctorate.

But always at the front of his mind there festered the knowledge that these events had taken place a long time ago. They had all occurred within a period of eight years, and since then nearly the same period had elapsed, and in all that time nothing had happened. Not a solitary highlight. This meant, among other things, that Hugh had developed a very confused sense of the passage of time: he was *aware* that eight years had passed since he had received his final degree, but because there were no landmarks to punctuate these years, he could no longer distinguish them from one another, or achieve any grasp of their cumulative span. That day of triumph in Coventry cathedral seemed neither recent nor distant; it seemed, if anything, to belong to a quite different level of existence. His life now comprised other realities: the hiss of the gas fire and the heavy warmth of his bedroom; the texture of pubic hair as he twined it around his index finger; the smell (to which he had long since become immune) of the unwashed socks and under-pants stashed under the bed; and the daily routine of forcing himself, at about 2.30, out of his bed, out of the flat, onto a bus and onto the university campus, in search of a kind of companionship.

Three o'clock found him walking through the rain to the bus station at Pool Meadow. There was an icy wind and in the distance, from the precinct, he could hear Christmas carols being played over a tannoy system. This reminded him that soon he would have to go back and visit his family, choose cards and presents, and he scowled. They would ask him the usual questions – 'When are you going to get yourself a job?', 'Are you seeing anyone at the moment?' – and he would have to suffer the subtle taunts of his younger brother who sold bathroom fittings for a

184

company based in Aberdeen and made more money in a month than Hugh had ever earned in his life. But there would be decent meals and when it all got too much he could go up to his bedroom and smoke. Before anything else he would have to phone his parents and get them to send down the money for the rail fare home.

He was one of three passengers on the bus, and had the top deck to himself for the whole journey. At various stops he looked out for familiar faces – friends, lecturers, students who might have been staying up for part of the vacation – but none appeared; perhaps the weather was keeping them indoors. Similarly, there were no other customers in the coffee bar. Friday afternoons out of term were always quiet, but today there seemed to be a level of inactivity which unsettled even Hugh, accustomed as he was to the atmosphere of empty cafés and deserted bars. Sometimes he chatted to the woman who served behind the counter but he could tell that she wasn't in the mood this time; she was reading a magazine, and anyway he couldn't think of anything to say. So he sat and made his cup of hot chocolate last for nearly half an hour, until another customer finally appeared: it was Dr Corbett, the English department's recently appointed senior lecturer. Being, like most of the staff, on cordial terms with Hugh, he came over and joined him. He had a beard and a leather jacket and had bought himself some coffee and a piece of chocolate cake. They exchanged murmured greetings, after which Corbett began eating his cake and Hugh was able to come up with nothing more original than:

'Quiet today, isn't it?'

'Well, it's getting on for Christmas,' said the highly acclaimed author of *The Intelligent Heart: Thought and Feeling in the Eighteenth-Century Novel.*

'Been working on something today, have you?' Hugh asked. 'A new book or something?'

'Examiners' meeting,' said Corbett, with his mouth full. 'We had to fix the questions today, for next term's paper, on the poetry course.'

'That was today?' said Hugh, incredulous. 'Was Davis there?'

Corbett nodded.

'But he said he'd tell me when you were having that meeting,' said Hugh. 'He told me that I could come along. He said I could come along and make some suggestions. I'd worked out a question. I'd got this question all worked out. And it was today! Why didn't anyone tell me?'

'You couldn't really have come along,' said Corbett. 'It was just for the teaching staff.'

'So who set the question on Eliot?'

'Davis did.'

'Davis? But Davis doesn't know a thing about Eliot. He doesn't have the first faintest bloody idea about Eliot. What was his question?'

'I don't know. Something about *The Waste Land.*'

'But it's always *The Waste Land.* That's why I was going to come along. I'd got this brilliant question all worked out. It was all about "Little Gidding".'

Corbett smiled. 'Your pet subject.'

'Exactly. You know Malcolm Kirkby, do you?'

'Well, I've heard of him, yes.'

'Wrote that book about the *Four Quartets*?'

'Yes.'

'Well, you know what he said about me, don't you? In that book.'

'No.'

'Well, you know I had that thing published in *Notes and Queries*?'

'Did you?'

'It was about line 25 of "Little Gidding".'

'What was it – a note, or a query?'

'Well, it was a sort of note, I suppose. Anyway, do you know what he said about it in his book?'

'What?'

'He said it would never be possible to read that line in the same way again. Following my note. It's changed the whole thing, according to him.'

'That's quite a compliment.'

'So I know what I'm talking about. I'm telling you, I could set a better question than Davis, any day of the week.'

'Well, he's pretty much played out, that bloke, if you want my opinion. He'll be retiring in a year or two. He can't even remember what he's meant to be talking about, half the time. The students are always complaining about it.'

'So why's he still teaching? Why can't you get some new blood into the department? You're cutting your own throats, you know, because in ten years' time it's going to be dead from the neck up.'

'We don't have the money. Cutbacks, economies – we're all having to tighten our belts.' Corbett wiped away the last of the chocolate cake from the edges of his mouth, and added: 'It's no use getting angry about it. Universities have been overmanning themselves for years, just like industry.'

'Well, you can afford to say that, can't you?'

'It's not complacency, Hugh. It's realism,' said the distinguished editor of *Men and Mountains: Essays on the Political Commitment of the Artist*. 'I mean, I know all about the problems that people like yourself are facing these days. But look on the bright side.'

'There's a bright side? Tell me about it.'

'Well, at least you're over the first hurdle. At least you've got your Ph.D. A lot of people don't even get that far: they don't have the staying power. For instance – did you ever meet that friend of Robin's, Aparna? Aparna Indrani.'

'Yes, I met her a few times. Why?'

'Did you know she's left?'

'Left? When?'

'A couple of months ago, apparently. She never told *me* about it, or anybody else in the department, and I'm supposed to be her bloody supervisor. Just packed her bags and left. Left half of her stuff in store here, and nobody knows when she's going to come back and collect it. And not a word about finishing her thesis. Just dumped the whole lot in my pigeon-hole, without a note or anything. Didn't even take it with her.'

'So what's all that about?'

'Like I said, no staying power. I mean, she'd been messing around with the thing for nearly six years, and I'd been pretty patient with her, I can tell you. But there you are.'

'Incredible.'

'She just couldn't . . . get it all together,' said the author of the much-vaunted pamphlet, 'The Psychology of Female Creativity', recently published as part of the *Studies in Contemporary Aesthetics* series. 'Too screwed up with problems of her own, probably.'

They contemplated this diagnosis for a few moments.

'I never liked her that much, I must say,' said Hugh. 'She was a prickly woman. Always picking you up if you said something she didn't like. In a way you'd expect her to leave in a huff like that.'

'Well, it's no skin off my nose,' said Corbett. 'At least I don't have to read the stuff any more.'

A lone student arrived at the periphery of the café, took a slow, mournful look around, and left. Hugh went over to the serving counter to order two coffees, but the woman was nowhere to be seen and his shouts of 'Hello' in the direction of the kitchen went unanswered.

'She'll probably be back in a minute,' he said, returning to the table. He was still thinking about Aparna. 'Perhaps she was upset about what happened to Robin.'

'Maybe. I heard – I mean, probably it was just a rumour – but I heard that they were having some sort of affair.'

'Almost certainly, I should think. They were seeing each other all the time, towards the end. I can't be sure, because

Robin never used to confide in me about things like that. I don't know why – I was his friend, after all. But he could be pretty stand-offish when it suited him. I suppose he was just another of these people with no staying power. Only in a rather more extreme sense.'

'Well, who knows what goes on inside the head of a bloke like that.'

'I think frustration with work had a lot to do with it,' said Hugh. 'He wasn't getting anywhere with his thesis. Even I could see that.'

'The guy was off his trolley, basically,' said Corbett, whose series of lectures on the relationships between madness and intellectual achievement had been one of the highlights of the autumn term. 'We don't have to make excuses. Mind you, as far as his work went, I should think that being supervised by Davis would have been enough to send anyone round the twist.'

'I gather he's not the most dynamic of supervisors. They only ever met up about once a year, or something.'

'He's out of order. Past it. The sooner we can persuade him to pack it in, the better it'll be for everybody.'

At this point Professor Davis himself wandered into the café, carrying a battered old briefcase and wiping his spectacles with a dirty handkerchief. After spotting Hugh and Dr Corbett, and after some brief hesitation, he came to join them. Corbett fetched him a chair and Hugh insisted on buying him some coffee and a macaroon. There was a long pause while he struggled to get the lid off his plastic carton of cream, sugared the coffee, ate about half of the cake and blew his nose. Then, looking thoughtful, he remarked:

'Very wet, today.'

Hugh nodded in attentive agreement.

'Outside,' Davis added, to clear up any ambiguity.

'Absolutely.'

'On a day like this,' said Davis, weighing his words with extreme care, 'you need an umbrella.'

'Or an anorak,' said Corbett. 'An anorak with a hood.'

'Quite.'

He took a sip of coffee, and decided to add another lump of sugar.

'Still,' said Hugh, 'it's nearly Christmas.'

'True,' said Professor Davis. 'Very true. The end of another year. Time marches on.'

'It seems to have gone very quickly, this year,' said Corbett.

'I think it's gone slowly,' said Hugh.

'These things are relative,' said Davis, 'in the long run. A year only seems long if a lot has happened in it. I would say that quite a lot has happened, in the last year.'

'Do you mean globally,' said Hugh, 'or locally?'

'Both,' said Davis. 'There was Westland. There was Libya. There was Chernobyl. There was that nasty leak in the roof of the Staff Club dining room.'

'And there was Robin,' said Dr Corbett.

'Precisely. There was Robin.'

A respectful silence ensued.

'Hugh and I were wondering,' said Corbett, 'whether

the real problem with Robin was his work. Did anyone ever see his work, apart from you? Was it any good?'

'What was it *about*, Robin's thesis?'

'Well,' said Professor Davis, 'it covered a wide range of literary topics, from a variety of different viewpoints.'

'Would you say his approach was . . . theoretical?'

'It could have been described as theoretical, yes.'

'Rather than practical?'

'It could also have been described as practical, I suppose.'

'Would you say his methodology was . . . Marxist?'

'It had elements of Marxism, undoubtedly.'

'As opposed to formalist?'

'But he had certain formalist leanings, it has to be said.'

'Did he confine his researches to a particular author, or a particular period?'

'He might have done, in the fullness of time. You see, his work never really took shape. He had difficulty getting his thoughts down on paper.'

'Did you ever read any of his stories?' asked Hugh, and they both turned to look at him in surprise.

'He wrote stories?'

'Yes. He had these illusions about wanting to be a writer. He didn't use to talk about them much, but one night when we both got drunk back at his place he showed me these stories he'd written. I read them all.'

'What sort of stories were they?'

'Short stories.'

'And did they tell you anything about him? Did they help you to understand him?'

Hugh considered.

'Not really.'

'What were they about?'

'You see, I can't see the point of trying to *understand* these things anyway,' said Hugh. 'I mean, what's the point? It's not going to change anything, is it? That's what I keep saying to Emma: "Look, it's not going to *change* anything, even if you find out why he did it. So what?"'

'Who's Emma?' Corbett asked.

'She was his lawyer.'

'You're still in touch with her, are you?' said Davis. 'I thought she left Coventry months ago.'

'She came back. I don't know whether she's still working here or what. Anyway she keeps phoning me up and asking questions about Robin. I suppose she feels guilty about it or something: she seems to want to rake the whole thing up again.'

'There was an interview with the boy's father in the evening paper recently,' said Davis. 'Apparently Robin's family have been writing letters to him, holding him responsible for what happened. It seems rather unreasonable to me.'

'It's the same thing again,' said Hugh. 'There's no point in trying to get at the truth behind all that. It doesn't matter whether Robin actually did it or not. The point is that he *could* have done it. He was capable of it.'

'What do you mean, capable of it?'

'Well, he had some very strange ideas about sex. That *is* clear from the stories, if nothing else.'

'Strange ideas?' said Dr Corbett, leaning forward.

'It's just that . . . men and women . . . going out together: I don't think he thought it was a very good idea.'

'How extraordinary,' said Professor Davis.

'He had all these affairs,' said Hugh, 'and they never lasted very long. I don't know what he used to do to those women, but . . . it makes you wonder, doesn't it?'

Professor Davis and Dr Corbett wondered, silently and in unison. Then Corbett said:

'This Emma woman – she keeps ringing you up, does she?'

'Yes. Three or four times in the last week.'

'I wonder why.'

'I told you, she's got this obsession with Robin. A few weeks ago I came across this thing he wrote, something he lent me, and she says she wants to read it.'

'What is it?'

'It's just a copy of his last story. One of the last things he did, apparently, was to throw all his stuff away, but there were these four stories which he was writing in different notebooks. Emma's still got one of them – the second, I think – and I've got the fourth. It's just a little story with some notes scribbled at the end of it. They're not very interesting, I keep telling her. Anyway, she's going to come over and see it.'

'What, to your place?'

'Yes, tomorrow night.'

The professor and the doctor exchanged meaningful glances.

'Didn't she leave her husband?' Davis asked.

'That's right.'

'How long have you known her?' Corbett asked.

'Quite a while – about four years. Why? What are you suggesting?'

But Dr Corbett simply looked at his watch and stood up.

'I've really got to be getting along,' he said. 'Joyce will be wanting to get the dinner ready soon. I'll be seeing you both next term, no doubt. Have a happy Christmas, Leonard.' He put his hand on Hugh's shoulder. 'Good luck for tomorrow, then. Try and make it a Happy New Year.'

Then he was gone and Hugh was staring after him in puzzlement.

'That was a weird thing to say.'

'Norman's mind tends to run in rather set patterns,' explained Professor Davis. 'I think he assumed that your playing host tomorrow night to a young, attractive, unattached lady could only mean one thing.'

He shook his head. 'He's wrong.'

'You mean she's not so attractive?' said Davis, attempting to sip from an empty coffee cup.

'Not at all. She's very attractive. But all the same . . .'

Davis chuckled, replaced the cup, and rose to his feet. He picked up his briefcase and brushed crumbs from his corduroy jacket.

'Look, Hugh,' he said, 'you don't want to live alone all your life, do you? In a bedsit? Let yourself go. It's Christmas.'

Hugh did not answer, until, as Davis was walking away,

he called out, 'Why didn't you tell me about the meeting today?' But the professor's hearing was not all that it used to be.

*

Hugh got soaked again on the way home and was shivering violently by the time he got back to his room. On the radio the weatherman predicted that the rain would turn to hail or snow overnight. He lay in the bath that evening for more than an hour, until the water was quite cold. He started to make plans for Emma's visit. He would cook an elaborate meal, maybe something Mexican, and he would tidy up the room properly, leaving the windows open all morning while he was down at the launderette and the supermarket. It felt good to be making plans again. Now that he had had time to think about them, Corbett's words no longer seemed so foolish: it was true that Emma had been phoning him a lot recently, and hadn't she made a special effort to come to his birthday party, back in the summer? Probably, like him, she was simply lonely and a little physical affection just before Christmas was exactly what she needed.

He went straight from the bath into bed but found, as usual, that he couldn't sleep. The ordinary dull fantasies went through his mind, as well as distorted fragments of the day's conversation and some thoughts about the things he would say tomorrow. At one point he realized that he no longer knew where to find his copy of Robin's story. In a panic he switched the bedside light on, got up, and began to search, naked, for the small red notebook; when he found it he felt more wakeful than ever and decided to read the whole story again. It wasn't very long.

There was absolute silence in Hugh's room as he read, and it was a silence which he knew only too well. He knew that there is no hush quite as deathly as the one you get in the hour before dawn, when you are alone in bed, and the light is on; and there is nothing which makes you hear this silence more acutely than the knowledge that snow has started to fall through the night outside your window.

4. *The Unlucky Man*

In the tea room of a hotel in a provincial spa town, a
string quartet is playing a melancholy tango.

A man was sitting alone at a table by the window. Some
of the time he was listening to the music, some of the
time he was looking out at the street, some of the time
he was anxiously searching the faces of the other patrons.
Most of the time he stared blankly in front of him. He
was very depressed. He was an estate agent (reason
enough to be depressed already, you might have thought,
but not the whole story, as will be revealed) and he
should have been at work that afternoon, but the impetus
to carry on with his life had deserted him. The
foundations of his existence had started to crumble. His
presence in the tea room was merely a last stand, a final
desperate effort to regain some sort of control; to impose
a kind of justice. But, as he looked at his watch, looked
at the door, looked out at the street, he began to suspect
that even here he had miscalculated.

Suddenly he became aware that a man was standing
over him, smiling down at him. For a moment he did
not recognise the face, and then the name, the features

and the associated memories slowly cohered. He too broke into an unexpected smile.

'Larry Norden!' he said.

'Harry Eatwell!'

'Well, for goodness' sake! Sit down, sit down.'

'I'm not disturbing you?'

'No, not at all.'

Harry and Larry had last seen each other some eight years before, when they had been at school together. They had never been particularly good friends, but these things tend to get forgotten on occasions like this, amid the glow of nostalgia and the excitement of a coincidental meeting.

'So what brings you here?'

'Well, I live here,' said Harry. 'I live and work in this town now. How about you?'

'Oh, I spend some time in this area, now and again. Seeing friends. So – how did things turn out for you?'

'Oh, not so bad, I've done OK.'

'Everything worked out the way you planned, did it?'

There was a slightly ironic inflexion to this question which made Harry ask, 'What do you mean?'

'I was just thinking of what you used to be like at school. You were always so damn organized. I remember – what were we, eighteen? – when you had your whole life planned out. Do you remember how we used to talk about our ambitions, how we wanted our lives to turn out? Those discussions we used to have?'

'I remember them well.'

'And did it all come true? You said that by the time you were twenty-five you wanted to be an estate agent, and to be married, and to have your own home, and a sports car?'

'Well, here I am: I'm an estate agent, and I'm married, and I've got a wife and a car. It's all come true.'

'That's amazing.'

'And how about you? You said you wanted to be . . . a long-distance lorry driver! With an apartment in Spain and a novel published under your own name.'

'That's right.'

'And has it happened?'

'No, I'm the marketing officer for a basket factory just outside Ashby-de-la-Zouch.'

'Oh.' Harry's voice betrayed a real disappointment. 'Still, I suppose you're happily married now, eh?'

'No.'

'Or you're engaged to some lovely girl?'

'No.' He patted Harry on the back. 'You needn't worry about me, you know. It's always been the same with me: easy come, easy go. Take life as it comes. No worries. Now you – ' He sat back and looked him in the eye ' – I'd say that you had worries.'

Harry looked undecided for a few seconds, as if he was trying to pull a brave face together. Then he gave up.

'I can't hide it from you. You've caught me at a very bad time. Everything's gone wrong recently.'

'Tell me about it, Harry.'

Harry drank some mineral water and wiped his brow; he didn't seem to know how to begin.

'Well – you know how it is when you feel completely in control of your life? When you hold all the threads?'

'No. I don't think I've ever had that feeling.'

'Yes, but you know how it is when you trust someone? When you know how things *are* with someone, even when you're away from them. Like . . . like when you're a little kid, and you're tucked up in bed and you're sleeping like a light, and the reason you're sleeping so well is that you know your parents are downstairs and watching the TV and thinking about you, and everything's OK.'

'Well, actually, my parents were always either fighting with each other or having sex. But anyway, go on.'

'Well, my life's always been like that, you see. I've always *known*. The people I've been close to – I've never allowed them to surprise me. It's so important, that, isn't it? Otherwise life just becomes a sort of anarchy. It's always been so important to me that I know, for instance, at five o'clock, when I'm just seeing my last client, that Angela is back at home in the kitchen getting ready to put the casserole on. They're what keep me going, these little certainties.'

'And something's happened to disrupt all this?'

Harry's voice started to quiver. 'I found out that she's being unfaithful to me.'

He took another drink, while his friend leaned forward, put a hand on his arm, and said:

'You'd better tell me the whole story.'

★

Harry's suspicions had started when a colleague of his informed him, quite casually, that his wife had been seen in the hotel tea room at four o'clock one Wednesday afternoon. Harry knew that this was impossible, because his wife invariably stayed at home in the afternoons, listening to the play on Radio 4. Indeed on that very Wednesday evening she had described the plot of this play to him in some detail over dinner, although he later found out that her synopsis was lifted word for word from the *Radio Times*. Anyway, at first he did not take the incident seriously; but when his colleague, reluctantly, told him that his wife had been seen with another man, and behaving in a way which suggested intimacy, Harry began to look worried.

'What do you think I should do?' he asked.

'You're in luck,' said the colleague. 'I can put you in touch with just the chap. A sort of detective. Very discreet, and very amenable. Specializes in this kind of work. I'll give you his card, and you can get in touch with him right away.'

Harry was given the address of an office at the top of a mews building at the cheap end of town. The name on the doorbell was 'Vernon Humpage'.

Mr Humpage turned out to be a balding, rather doleful man; he bore a certain resemblance to the character played by Mervyn Johns in *Dead of Night*. He quickly put Harry at his ease and explained that his work could be divided into two categories – research, and surveillance. In this particular case, he suggested, it might be well to

consider both. Harry agreed. Mr Humpage then promised
to provide him with a full report within the space of
seven days.

Their next meeting took place one week later.

'I've managed to find out a great deal, Mr Eatwell,'
said the detective.

'I'm pleased to hear it. Do call me Harold.'

'Gladly. Could I start by asking you a few questions?'

'Fire away.'

'When did you first meet your wife?'

'About two years ago.'

'I see: just after she got back from Berlin.'

'I'm sorry?'

'You know that your wife worked as a nightclub hostess
in Berlin for six months?'

'No.'

'She ran away there. Shortly after the divorce.'

'Divorce?'

'She's been married before, of course, but you knew
that. Actually my researches show that the marriage was
never officially dissolved; but he doesn't get out of prison
for another four years, so we don't have to worry about
that just yet.'

'Mr Humpage, I didn't know any of this,' said Harry,
his face loose with astonishment.

'Well, let's move on to surveillance. Harold, would you
say you had an accurate idea of how your wife spends
her time during the day?'

'Yes, I would.'

'Based on what?'

'Based on what she tells me.'

'All right, well, let's see now.' He picked up a handwritten sheet of paper from his desk. 'What's the first thing she does in the morning?'

'She, erm, she makes me a cup of tea.'

'That's correct. And then what?'

'And then we have breakfast together, and I go out to work.'

'Also correct.'

'Then she cleans up the kitchen and dusts downstairs.'

'No, I'm afraid she doesn't. The first thing she does after you leave the house in the morning is put her feet up, pour herself a gin and tonic, and have a smoke.'

'A smoke? My wife doesn't smoke.'

'Oh yes she does. Havana cigars. You didn't know that? Well, anyway: it then gets to be around mid-morning. You know what she does then?'

'Well, I've always pictured her having some coffee and biscuits . . . maybe drawing up a shopping list, watching some daytime television.'

'Wrong, I'm afraid. She phones her stockbroker.'

'Her stockbroker?'

'Yes. She has equity interests in five major light industrial businesses. A lot of buying and selling takes place. She didn't tell you?'

'No.'

'How odd. You know about the lunchtimes, of course.'

'Well, she's on this diet. She usually watches the news and has a light salad with some fruit juice. Doesn't she?'

'Actually she frequents a variety of local pubs. Yesterday it was The Bull and Gate: she had steak and kidney pie and chips and two pints of Yorkshire bitter. The day before that it was a wine bar in Dale Street: she had a double helping of chilli con carne and several whiskies. Sometimes she goes on her own, sometimes with friends.'

'But when does she find time to cook dinner? Surely it must take her most of the afternoon to cook those fabulous dinners.'

'Most of them are from packets. She usually pops in and gets them on her way back from the arcades.'

'The arcades?'

'She plays the machines. Three days out of the last four, she's been out working the fruit machines. Not too bad at it: usually comes out with more than she takes in.' He stopped and looked up. 'Is this disturbing you, Mr Eatwell?'

Harry had put on his overcoat, and was standing by the window.

'What then?' he asked. 'The hotel?'

Mr Humpage nodded.

'What time?'

'Four o'clock.'

Harry made for the door. 'I don't want to hear any more,' he said, but asked, as an afterthought, 'Is it always the same man?'

Humpage nodded again. And just as his client was leaving, he said, kindly: 'Harold.' Harry turned. 'No one has the right to control another person, you know.'

'He was right.'

'I suppose he was.'

Harold forced a smile and wiped his eyes. His old friend, who had been listening carefully, thought for some time before saying:

'Do you mind if I make some very personal remarks?'

'No, not really.'

'You see, frankly, Harry, I don't think you loved your wife at all. I think you loved what she stood for – or what you *made* her stand for.'

'How do you mean?'

'I mean that what's upsetting you isn't just the fact that your wife's been unfaithful. Your whole way of looking at the world – it's been shot to bits. And not before time. You can't make assumptions like that. You can't assume that people will always behave in the way you want them to. Life is chaotic. It's random. Have you only just noticed?'

'Is there nothing we can do, nothing at all, which proves we have control over our own lives?'

There was a short silence.

'Which way did you walk to the hotel?'

'By the river,' said Harry, not even registering any surprise at the question.

'And what were you thinking, while you were walking by the river?'

'I looked at it,' said Harry, 'and wondered how deep it was in the middle . . .'

'So there's your answer,' said his friend. 'It's the only way. If you really want to prove that *you* have control over what becomes of you, if you really want to break the vicious circle, that's how you do it.' He laughed, and patted Harry on the back. 'But that's not what you want – really – is it?'

Harry smiled back gratefully and shook his head.

'What you really want is a good cup of tea, and for someone to tell those guys to play something more cheerful. So why don't I go and do that?'

'All right, Larry. Thanks.'

Harry went to the lavatory, washed his hands and face in warm water, and stood for a while with his back to the wall, breathing deeply. He had thought that he would cry, he had even wanted to cry, but the tears had failed him. Instead he felt a subtle elation which, had he been capable of analysing it, he might have recognised as a return of his own deadly self-reassurance. What he found peculiarly comforting at that moment was the thought of Larry buying him another cup of tea, waiting for him, thinking up further words of consolation and encouragement. He was pleased to feel that he was again occupying centre-stage in the consciousness of another human being.

It was just as well, then, that he was not there to see Angela arrive at their table, murmur 'Lawrence, darling', run her hand through his hair and kiss him on the mouth. By the time Harry emerged from the lavatory, they had both disappeared.

Emma sank into the sofa and looked around the sitting room of her little house. It was not that she was tired, or that she especially wanted to take stock of her sitting room at that moment, but she had got herself ready too early, as usual, and now she had time to kill. She liked this room. You entered it straight from the street and dinner guests always began by saying, 'Oh, what a lovely room.' Then they noticed the photographs arranged in groups of four on the walls: sepia prints of Emma's great-grandparents and their family, taken near the turn of the century – she had brought them back down from Edinburgh that summer. She looked at them now and felt supported by their benign melancholy, the fixed, unforced confidence of their gaze. In the face of a sad, upright great-great-aunt she could discern a curious resemblance to herself. Up in the attic at home, while they had been hunting these photographs out one afternoon from damp cardboard boxes, her father had told her the history of this woman, as well as he could remember it: she had married young and was widowed young and had never had children. Quite late in life she had taken to medicine and had even published a now forgotten textbook.

Emma felt comfortable sitting on the sofa looking at her family portraits, and suddenly it occurred to her that she did not want to go out this evening at all. This invariably happened. She worried herself with fears that she would never be able to build up a proper social life and then, when the opportunity finally arose to get out and see somebody, she had qualms. She hadn't been out all day and first there would be the problem of wiping all the snow off the car and getting it started. Then she would have to stop off at an off-licence and get some wine, and then she would have the worry of leaving her car parked out in the street near Hugh's flat, which was not in a particularly safe area. And once she was there she wouldn't be able to drink much herself, because she would have to drive back. All but the main roads were bound to be slippery and dangerous. On top of all this, did she really want to spend a whole evening with Hugh, whose company, she now realized, she had mainly used to enjoy as an antidote to her husband's?

Probably she would have had no hesitation in cancelling the evening if it were not for her anxiety to gain further information about Robin. Even if the story which Hugh had in his possession turned out to be unimportant, there was a peculiar pleasure in the prospect simply of spending a few hours talking about him. She had not yet asked herself why it was that she wanted to find out more about the circumstances of his death, or when it was that her initial, frozen shock had developed into a more enquiring kind of involvement. It had taken nearly a month, since the idea had first suggested itself, to compose her letter to Ted. He had written back promptly and courteously. He had been appalled, he said, by the news of the suicide, and he could sympathize with her feelings of implication and grief. Nevertheless, he thought it absurd that any blame should attach to Emma herself. If he could set her mind at rest by offering any sort of explanation, he would do so, but he felt as baffled by the whole affair as she did. Nothing that had passed between him and Robin on the day of their last meeting had prepared him for such a development. They had ended by swapping reminiscences of their undergraduate days, in the most affectionate terms. Ted was deeply sorry that he could be of no further assistance; but he took this opportunity of returning to her a notebook, belonging to Robin, which he had found in the pocket of his overcoat some weeks before. It contained the first of his short stories. Ted must have taken it home with him by mistake.

He had also sent her a Christmas card, and a photocopied newsletter giving her a great deal of irrelevant information about his family. The card stood on the mantelpiece with six others: there would be fewer than usual this year. Two of her friends had invited her to come and stay with them for Christmas Day, and while Emma duly recognized the kindness behind these offers, she resented the underlying assumption that to be separated from one's husband was to be reduced to a state of chronic isolation and possibly homelessness. The idea of spending Christmas alone did not worry her, although she had decided, mainly in response to pressure from her parents, to go back to Edinburgh for a few days. Meanwhile she had succeeded in making her house, downstairs at least, look tolerably festive. She noticed that the tree in the stairwell had been shedding its needles again, and was glad of the excuse to get the vacuum cleaner out and busy herself for a few minutes. When that was finished she decided that she might as well go.

There were very few people in the streets, for a Saturday night. Humanity made its presence felt in Coventry that evening not by walking drunkenly along pavements, or making its way, in groups of four or five, to wine bars and nightclubs; rather, it implied itself by means of lit windows, drawn curtains, distant music. Behind every front door Emma could imagine parties in progress, televisions being watched, drinks being poured and children staying up late. She wondered what Mark and Elizabeth would be doing; at least, she assumed that Mark and Elizabeth would be together that night, somewhere or other. When Mark and Emma had separated, they had made the usual promises of continuing to see each other as friends, but because they had ceased to be friends long ago, long before they split up, these promises had never been kept. She had very little idea of how he spent his time these days, and was unable completely to subdue her curiosity on the subject. Naturally they had sent each other Christmas cards.

Emma parked beneath an amber streetlamp a few doors away from Hugh's flat. By now the roads were layered with more than an inch of snow, and he seemed a long time answering the doorbell, long enough for her to get thoroughly cold. When he appeared, he was apologetic.

'I've been having a bit of trouble with the entrée,' he explained. 'I seem to have gone a bit berserk with the pepper.'

'Hello,' said Emma. 'I brought you this.'

She handed him a bottle, wrapped in purple paper.

'Hello,' he said. 'Thank you.' He gave her a hairy kiss on the cheek.

She followed him up the stairs, wondering why he was wearing a tie.

'I'm afraid the main course is going to be a bit late,' he said, ushering her into his room. 'The people across the landing have been doing jacket potatoes and I've only just been able to get at the oven.'

'That's all right. I didn't realize you had to share your kitchen.'

'Well, it's not usually a problem. Are you going to sit down?'

Emma found that she had the option either of taking her place at the table straight away, or sitting on the bed, which was neatly made and covered with a dull green bedspread. Postponing the decision, she strolled over to the bookcase and started looking at the titles. It had always fascinated her that Hugh, who lived permanently either on or just below the poverty line, should spend so much money on books, and also on books which seemed so militantly abstruse and specialized. Works of literary theory stood side by side with modernist novels in the original French, and there were smatterings of music criticism and medieval English poetry.

'Do you ever read these books?' she asked.

'Well, only some of them, obviously,' said Hugh, who was in the middle of opening a bottle, a process which he now interrupted in order to show her a particularly bulky paperback which had been lying on his dressing table. 'It's just nice to know they're around. Here – have a look at this: I got it earlier this week. I'll just go and fetch the glasses.'

Emma couldn't make head or tail of the book, but she sat on the bed and left it politely open on her lap while waiting for Hugh to return.

'It's good, this, is it?' she said.

'Actually, I was a little disappointed,' said Hugh, handing her a full glass. 'Cheers. Your very good health. Normally you can expect Fournier to be fairly progressive, as far as narratology's concerned, but I think he's developing revisionist tendencies.'

'I see,' said Emma. 'That's a pity.'

'These things happen,' said Hugh.

'Life goes on, I suppose. Society won't crumble at its foundations.'

'Exactly.' He took the book from her hands, slightly irritated that her irony had crept up on him like that, without his noticing. 'Nice wine,' he said.

'Thank you.'

'So.' Hugh looked round the room, looked at the two empty chairs, looked at the space on the bed. 'Do you mind if I sit beside you?'

'Not at all.'

He sat beside her. The bed was against the wall, which permitted him to lean back, although Emma continued to sit forward.

'Don't you think the table looks nice?' he asked, brightly.

From somewhere or other he had produced matching silver cutlery, two Stuart crystal wine glasses, cotton napkins and table mats depicting hunting scenes. There was also a candle, as yet unlit, and a small vase of flowers.

'It looks lovely,' said Emma. 'I'd no idea I was going to be made such a fuss of.'

'Well, everybody needs cheering up, now and again, don't they?' said Hugh.

'You think I need cheering up?'

'No, I mean it cheered *me* up, getting it all ready. It's nice to make a bit of an effort.'

'Don't you enjoy cooking for yourself? I do.'

'You haven't had time to get used to it,' said Hugh. 'I found that the novelty started to wear off after the first four and a half years or so.'

'You mean you still haven't found yourself a girlfriend?' said Emma. She had decided that she was in a teasing mood.

'I think it's time for the soup,' said Hugh.

He went into the kitchen. Emma lit the candle and took her place at the table.

'I was sorry to hear about you and Nick,' said Hugh, as he ladled chilled watercress soup into her bowl.

'Mark,' said Emma. 'My husband's name is Mark.'

'Sorry. Of course. Anyway – I was sorry to hear about it. You must feel . . . well, it must all have been a bit of a shock.'

'Not really. I'm surprised by how quickly I've adjusted to it.'

'Where are you living now?'

'I've bought myself a house. Just a little terrace. I've been doing it up for the last couple of months, and that's kept me busy. This is very nice.'

'Not too peppery?'

'No.' She stopped eating, and considered. 'Perhaps it'll really hit me, in a little while.'

Hugh, who did not know whether she was referring to the pepper or her separation, waited for her to elaborate.

'I mean, I was cutting it fine as it was. Having children, I mean.' She sighed. 'I really did want them, too.'

'Did?'

'Well, I'm trying not to think about it just now. There's no point, at the moment.'

'Bread rolls,' said Hugh. 'I forgot the bread rolls.' He went to the kitchen again and was back very quickly, saying as he returned: 'Of course, I've always wanted children. I'm very good with them, you see. It's something that comes quite naturally to me. I've already got a nephew and a niece. Yes, they love to see their Uncle Hugh. It's no substitute for having your own, though. I don't suppose I'll leave it long before I settle down, now. I don't want to go on like this all my life.'

'You sound very confident,' said Emma, smiling. 'Do you feel you have the means to settle down?'

'Not at the moment, no, obviously. I've got prospects, though.'

'Such as?'

'Well, I was talking to one of the senior lecturers the other day, and it seems pretty clear that Professor Davis – he's the head of the department – it seems pretty clear that he'll be retiring quite soon.'

'You're suggesting that you're going to be appointed head of the English department?'

'No, obviously that would be unrealistic. But there's going to have to be a bit of a shuffle. There's bound to be a vacancy, somewhere along the line. And my face is pretty well known around that department.'

'You consider that an advantage.'

Hugh held her gaze for a moment and then tapped the side of the bowl with his soup spoon.

'I'll just go and check on the potatoes,' he said.

He had been forced to abandon the Mexican meal, not having allowed enough time to round up the ingredients. The next course consisted of strips of pork, served in a sauce of cream and cider. By the time it was on the table, Emma had steered the conversation around to Robin.

'I really never imagined he'd do anything like that,' she

was saying. 'I had no idea. I didn't even think it would cross his mind.'

'Well, you hardly knew him, did you? I thought you only met him once or twice.'

'But that's exactly what's so upsetting: for me, as a lawyer. You spend an hour or more talking to a client – and you can find out a lot about a person in an hour, if it's to the point – and you come away thinking that you know them: thinking that you've got the basis of an understanding. This is a caring profession, as far as I'm concerned. Otherwise I don't want to be in it. But then you realize – it's nothing. Nothing. You've barely scratched the surface. You've found out just enough to get involved, just enough to be upset when the thing goes wrong, but not enough to understand the kind of help that was needed.'

'Robin didn't need help.'

'How can you say that?'

'I mean, there was nothing anyone could do. And as soon as we start thinking that there was, then we're just going to go around spending the rest of our lives feeling guilty about it.'

'And shouldn't we feel guilty?'

'How's your pork?'

Emma hesitated, wondering whether she should let the subject drop so easily.

'It's delicious, quite delicious,' she said. 'But it's getting a bit hot in here.'

'Take your jumper off.'

Emma took her jumper off, and folded it carefully on

the bed beside her coat. Hugh turned the gas fire down.

'All these questions you're asking,' he said, 'writing to Ted, visiting me – if you're just doing it to stop yourself feeling guilty, forget it. I don't think it had anything to do with why he killed himself. The charge, I mean.'

'What makes you think that?'

'Because after it had happened, after he'd been charged, he seemed perfectly happy. He even seemed to cheer up a bit. If he was really depressed, it was *before* then. That's what I think, anyway.'

'I don't know,' said Emma sadly. 'I don't know why I'm doing it. It just upset me so much. I didn't even know him. *You* must have been devastated.'

'It was a bit of a turn-up, I must say,' said Hugh, pouring more wine for both of them. 'You know, the person you should really talk to is Aparna; but she's left, apparently. Fled the country.' He stopped, the bottle in mid-air, pensive, and then resumed pouring, shaking his head. 'No, that's a stupid idea.'

'What is?'

'You never met her, did you?'

'No. What were you thinking?'

'I just wondered . . . I mean, two people, alone together in a flat on the fourteenth floor of a tower block: nobody knows what was going on, do they? She was a volatile woman. Perhaps there was an argument, he did something to offend her, there was a struggle . . . who knows?'

Emma seemed unconvinced.

'You promised to show me the last story,' she said.

'In a minute,' said Hugh. 'Are you ready for some fruit?'

They had fresh pineapple, satsumas and cheese and biscuits. Hugh made some coffee, and resumed his position on the bed. Emma remained at the table.

'Are you comfortable over there?'

'Fine, thank you.'

'Is it still too warm for you?'

'No, I'm fine.'

He began to wonder if there was any chance of getting her talking about a subject other than Robin. In desperation, he said:

'So what do you think of this flat, then?'

'It's very nice. Don't you like it?'

'No, I'm bored with living here. I'm thinking of moving.' There was a longish silence. 'Is it big, your new house?'

'No, it's just a little house.'

'Just right for one, is it? Or is there room for someone else?'

'Hugh, I didn't realize how late it was getting,' said Emma, looking at her watch. 'It's been a lovely meal, it really has. It's going to take me a while to get home, with the roads and everything. Can I see the story now?'

He got up and pointed to his bedside table.

'There it is,' he said. 'I'll make a start on the washing-up while you're reading it.'

He left the room. Emma carried her cup of coffee over to the bed and sat down. She held the notebook against her open palm for a while. Then she turned the pages carefully and began to read as fast as the untidy handwriting would allow.

After about fifteen minutes Hugh returned and sat on the bed beside her. Emma seemed to have finished reading: she was staring thoughtfully at the last page.

'Well, are you any the wiser?' he asked, leaning back against the wall.

'Yes,' said Emma, 'I think so. These things were obviously on his mind. That moment, when Lawrence says that killing yourself is a good idea, because it shows that you have control over your own life . . . Isn't that relevant to what Robin did?'

Hugh shook his head.

'He was just playing around. This is the least relevant of the stories to anything that Robin really thought. He'd lost interest by then. If he'd meant it to be serious he would have written it completely differently: which is more or less what he says there.'

He turned a page and pointed to some lines scribbled in pencil.

THIS STORY IS ALL WRONG, Robin had written.
Get rid of Humpage. Find a different device.
Humour inappropriate.
Keep basic plot but scrap last two paras and make whole story hinge on final conversation between Lawrence and Harold.
They discuss the merits of suicide in detail and at length.
Lawrence begins by quoting Simone Weil, as an illustration of their different approaches to life:

'Two ways of killing ourselves: suicide or detachment.'

'Who's that?' said Emma, indicating the unfamiliar name.

Hugh edged closer and peered at the handwriting.

'Some French woman,' he said. 'Let's have some more wine.'

'I'm driving,' said Emma, too late to stop him filling her glass.

'You don't have to.'

She did not notice that he had said this. The rest of Robin's notes appeared to have been added much later; they were in biro, and the writing was larger but even more difficult to decipher.

Further quotations from SW. (Is this what has happened?)
'For those whose "I" is dead we can do nothing, absolutely nothing. We never know, however, whether in a particular person the "I" is quite dead or only inanimate. If it is not quite dead, love can reanimate it as though by an injection, but it must be love which is utterly pure without the slightest trace of condescension, for the least shade of contempt drives towards death.'

'Emma,' said Hugh. 'Emma, look at me.'

'When the "I" is wounded from outside it starts by revolting in the most extreme and bitter manner like an animal at bay. But as soon as the "I" is half dead, it wants to be finished off

and allows itself to sink into unconsciousness. If it is then awakened by a touch of love, there is sharp pain which results in anger and sometimes hatred for whoever has provoked this pain. Hence the apparently

Here the writing ended. And as Emma was trying to understand these words, to think why Robin might have copied them down, she felt the touch of a hand on her shoulder. A hand was stroking her bare shoulder, inside her blouse. Then the weight of Hugh's body was against her and the hand was sliding downwards, down towards her breast. She pushed him away and stumbled to her feet.

'What do you think you're doing?' she asked, trying to quell the tremor in her voice.

Hugh didn't answer. She looked at him sternly, saw the need and the loneliness grained on his face, and could not find it in her to be angry.

'That's not why I came here. You must know that.'

He stood up, but came no closer. 'I'm sorry. It was a stupid thing to do. I didn't think.'

Emma pondered these words for a little while, then sighed. There seemed nothing more to say.

'I'd better go now.' She took her jumper and coat from the bed; drifted towards the door.

'No, Emma, please don't go. Please stay. I'm sorry. I told you – I wasn't thinking.'

She was already on the stairs now, but turned to reply, 'Then start thinking, Hugh. A little New Year's resolution, maybe – for both of us. Let's both start thinking now.'

Her voice barely reached him as she opened and closed the front door. When she had gone, Hugh took brief, rueful stock of the remains of their meal strewn over the table, then sank onto the bed, dizzy; bewildered at Emma, at Robin, at himself; his head throbbing with wine.

*

Sleep did not come easily to Emma that night, but when it came, it was deep and restful. She awoke to a brilliant midday light, flooding her bedroom, sheening the walls and the ceiling with a warm, clean white. She stretched slowly in the single bed, smothered in comfort; and the events of the previous night, when they began to resurface in her mind, seemed distant and unreal.

She had breakfast in the sunlit sitting room. The Sunday delivery had brought more cards, and it was not until she had finished with these and the memories they evoked that she found herself thinking of the words Robin had added to his last story. She could remember them only very indistinctly. She did not know what had happened to the notebook. She had meant to bring it away with her but presumably in her confusion she had left it with Hugh.

Emma was soon distracted from these thoughts by a commotion in the street outside her window. An engine was revving up loudly and persistently, spurred on by cries of encouragement from what sounded like a small crowd of people. She went to her front door and looked. Directly opposite her house, a van which had been parked on an incline overnight was stuck in the snow. The back wheels were spinning, and eight or nine people, including the neighbours from both sides, were trying to push it out.

'Do you need a hand?' she shouted, running over.

'We're nearly there, love,' said the man who lived in the house opposite Emma's, and whose son owned the van. 'One more push and we've done it.'

Amid a clamour of voices, laughter, instructions, panting and struggle, with the engine roaring and the wheels sending up fountains of snow into their faces, they heaved at the van and cheered as it swayed into motion. They watched as it toiled up the hill, and finally made it to the crest.

'Keep going, Ron!'

'Keep your revs up, son!'

Then they all clapped and cheered again as the van disappeared from view, billowing exhaust fumes.

The neighbours remained in a ragged group, chatting, their breath steaming in the air, arms folded, shifting from foot to foot in the cold.

'Everybody come inside,' said Ron's father. 'Come inside and have a drink.'

His wife saw that Emma was hesitating, standing uncertain at the edge of the road while the others kicked the snow off their shoes and started to go into the house. She took her gently by the arm and smiled at her.

'Come on, love,' she said. 'It'll warm you up.'

Emma was still dazzled by the sudden cold, the sunlight

reflected from the icy road and the back windows of the van, the surprising hilarity of the whole gathering. She had a vague recollection that she had been going to think about something important, before she had come outside.

'Thank you,' she said. 'Thanks, that would be lovely.'

POSTSCRIPT

by Aparna

Wednesday 28th October, 1987

Sometimes, after long absence, you return to a place which
has painful associations, and this can be an unpredictable
experience. You have certain expectations: that a particular
street, or room, or café, once revisited, will inspire a
particular feeling, and you are surprised when it fails to do
so. And what is still more surprising is the sudden pang of
memory provoked by scenes and locations which you
would never have credited with such power to wound. It
was like this when I returned to Coventry. All the places I
had dreaded seeing again – my flat, the streets through
which I had used to walk home from the bus, the university
campus where most of my belongings were stored – they
left me cold: I breezed in and out of them, level-headed
and resolute. But then in the afternoon, having an hour or
two to spare, we drove over to another part of town, where
Robin had lived. It was a more upmarket district altogether,
and in these neatly kept terraces and comfortable family
houses, the rather sad diffidence with which they took their
place in the world, I found echoes of Robin's melancholy

presence. It was a cold and sunny autumn day, a day of sharp outlines, and those streets seemed very real again: I had been beginning to hope that I had imagined them. We parked the car and I took Josef to see the front door of Robin's flat. It had been re-let; the new tenant came to the window and stared warily at us. There was very little I could say. I had told Josef the story already and he knew something of what I was thinking and he didn't try to break in upon my silences.

Several months after Robin died a Spanish student who had once been friendly with me at the university wrote me a letter inviting me to her wedding. I accepted the invitation and travelled to Spain, knowing that I would never come back to complete my studies. Borrowing money from my parents I then spent nearly ten weeks visiting Spain, France and Germany, which was where I met Josef. He was a good friend to me, bringing me much happiness, such happiness as I had never expected or even thought possible, after all I had been through, all I had seen. It surprises me that I do not think of him more often now. That day was our last day together, and it filled my head full of Robin, so that I had nothing to spare even for the pain of parting; but for this I think we were both grateful, in the end.

I have not made up my mind about Robin. I still don't know whether I could have helped him. I tried to show him kindness, although I realize now that I showed him too little, too late in the day. We should have spent less time talking and less time arguing and less time thinking about our books and more time thinking about each other. Perhaps we should have shared the same bed, and comforted each other in the night. But he was bad at choosing friends and should probably not have chosen me. As his friend I should have told him that nature never designed him for a separatist, that he would never have been made welcome by the people he admired, that the road he was travelling was merely the road to a lonely exile. Or somebody else should have told him this. One of his other friends.

Just as day was fading into twilight, we returned to the car and began the last stage of our journey together. As we drove out of Coventry I said my quiet farewells to this city which has been twice devastated, once by the bombs of a foreign army, once by the impact of a recession which was orchestrated by politicians, and which has bitten in the last few years, really bitten, spreading inertia and indifference, eating away at the work and the livelihood of the people. Yet these people remain cheerful and humorous; they look on the dark side of life but are no more complaining than any of their countrymen. I got the impression, when I was living there, that nobody was thinking very hard. And as I left, I wanted to wind down the window of Josef's car, and shout at the top of my voice: You should think, think, *think* about what is happening all around you. Think until your heads hurt with the effort and the worry of it. Thinking is not always dangerous, you know. It killed Robin but it will not kill you.

I didn't shout, anyway. It was a cold afternoon and we

kept the window of the car closed. It was cold on the plane, too, as it came in to land; when I first saw the lights of my city, a chill began to shake my whole body, and when I thought of the faces of my father and mother, it was with a mixture of longing and fear. I had not forgotten that home can be the strangest place of all.